James Hamblin Smith

Short Notes on the Greek Text

of the Acts of the apostles

James Hamblin Smith

Short Notes on the Greek Text
of the Acts of the apostles

ISBN/EAN: 9783337396848

Printed in Europe, USA, Canada, Australia, Japan

Cover: Foto ©Andreas Hilbeck / pixelio.de

More available books at **www.hansebooks.com**

SHORT NOTES

ON

THE GREEK TEXT

OF

THE ACTS OF THE APOSTLES

BY

J. HAMBLIN SMITH, M.A.

OF GONVILLE AND CAIUS COLLEGE
LATE LECTURER IN CLASSICS AT ST. PETER'S COLLEGE, CAMBRIDGE

FOURTH EDITION

RIVINGTONS

WATERLOO PLACE, LONDON

MDCCCXC

PREFACE.

THIS book is in the main a reprint of notes drawn up for the use of my own pupils in 1867.

Many references to Thucydides will be found in these notes; and for the following reason: it seems certain to me that the Author of the Acts was very familiar with certain parts of the History of Thucydides, and that much of what he read in Thucydides made a strong impression on his mind. I have no doubt whatever that he had studied with great care the whole of the Sixth Book of Thucydides; that he had read attentively a large portion of the Eighth Book; and that he was acquainted with some parts of the other Books. I have stated the reasons which have led me to this conclusion in a pamphlet, circulated privately in 1883. I will gladly send a copy of this pamphlet to any one who may desire to examine the evidence adduced by me in support of my opinion.

J. HAMBLIN SMITH.

CAMBRIDGE, 12th December, 1889.

INTRODUCTION.

1. THAT the writer of this treatise is identical with the author of the third Gospel is shown—

(1) By the testimony of early Christian writers, as Irenæus, Clemens Alexandrinus, and Tertullian.

(2) By the similarity of style and idiom observable in the books themselves, and in the usage of particular words.

(3) By the allusion in the first verse to the "former treatise" of the author.

2. The internal evidence with respect to the author of this work leads us to the following conclusions :—

(1) The writer was with St. Paul on his second journey, since in Acts xvi. 10 the *first person* is used for the first time in the narrative, proving that the writer accompanied St. Paul in his voyage to Macedonia.

(2) The writer accompanied St. Paul

to *Asia* (Acts xx. 6) ;
and to *Jerusalem* (Acts xx. 15) ;
and to *Caesarea* (Acts xxi. 8) ;
and to *Rome* (Acts xxviii. 16).

1

3. Of the personal history of St. Luke we know but little.

He is mentioned by name *three times* in St. Paul's Epistles, and in no other part of the New Testament.

Col. iv. 14. "Luke the beloved physician."

In this passage he is distinguished from "those of the circumcision," and hence we conclude that he was a *Gentile* by birth.

2 Tim. iv. 11. "Luke only is with me."

From this we infer that he continued with St. Paul to the end of his life.

Philemon 24. "Demas, Lucas, my fellow-labourers."

The name Lucas (*Λουκᾶς*) is an abbreviated form of Lucanus. Eusebius says he was born at Antioch. The date of his conversion is unknown; apparently he was not "an eye-witness and minister of the word from the beginning" (Luke i. 2). That he was taught the science of medicine is clear from Col. iv. 14; and a late tradition of the Church also declares that he was a painter of considerable skill.

4. This treatise is addressed to a person named Theophilus, to whom the Gospel of St. Luke is also addressed, but both works are clearly designed to instruct Christians of every class, whether Jews or Gentiles. The two chief subjects of this work are—

(1) The fulfilment of the promise of the Father by the descent of the Holy Spirit.

(2) The result of the outpouring of the Holy Spirit, by the dispersion of the Gospel among Jews and Gentiles.

"The book is intended to set forth the development of the Church from Jerusalem to Rome, from the metropolis of Judaism to the capital of the world, and therewith the transition of the Gospel from the Jews to the Gentiles, carried out under Divine guidance through the guilt of the former." — *Weiss.*

5. The period of time included in the Acts of the Apostles is somewhat more than thirty years, from the Resurrection of our Lord, A.D. 30, to the first imprisonment of St. Paul at Rome, A.D. 61—63.

Jerome states that the book was written at Rome between St. Paul's first and second imprisonments in that city, A.D. 63—65. But there is no certain evidence as to the place and time of writing.

6. The title prefixed to this treatise stands thus in the Vatican Manuscript—Πράξεις τῶν ἀποστόλων. The title in the Alexandrine Manuscript at the British Museum is Πράξεις τῶν ἁγίων ἀποστόλων.

CHAPTER I.

1. πρῶτον, *first*, put for πρότερον, *former.*

— ὧν, genitive by *attraction.*

— ἤρξατο ποιεῖν, *began to do*, equivalent to ἐποίησεν ἐν ἀρχῇ, *did in the beginning* of the process by which the Church was founded.

2. ἄχρι ἧς ἡμέρας, *till the day in which*, condensed for ἄχρι τῆς ἡμέρας ᾗ.

3. τεκμήριον means *a sure sign, a demonstrative proof*, stronger in meaning than σημεῖον.

3. δι᾽ ἡμερῶν τεσσαράκοντα, *during forty days.*

— τὰ περὶ τῆς βασιλείας τοῦ Θεοῦ, *the matters relating to the kingdom of God*, probably instructions by which the Apostles were guided in building up the Church.

4. συναλιζόμενος, *associating with.*

— ἣν ἠκούσατε, *which (said He) ye heard.* Notice the change from the indirect to the direct narration. Other instances will be found in xvii. 3, and xxiii. 22.

5. οὐ μετὰ πολλὰς ταύτας ἡμέρας, *after not many of these days*, i.e. after a few days including those just past. Comp. Terence Heaut. iv. 5, 4, *etsi scio hosce aliquot dies non sentiet.*

6. εἰ ἀποκαθιστάνεις; *dost thou intend to restore?* In late Greek εἰ was used as a regular interrogative particle. This use of εἰ originated in an ellipsis; *I should like to know, whether.*

7. ὑμῶν, genitive of *property* or *power.*

χρόνος implies an *indefinite* period of time.

καιρός is used for a *certain, fixed* season, *the right time*, the time suitable to the performance of anything.

8. When Christ sent the Apostles on their first mission (Matt. x. 5) He said, *Go not into the way of the Gentiles, and into any city of the Samaritans enter ye not: but go rather to the lost sheep of the house of Israel.*

This restriction He now removed.

9. ἐπήρθη, *He was taken up.*

— ὑπέλαβεν, *received and hid*, to give the force of the preposition.

10. ἀτενίζοντες, *looking steadfastly.* From ἀτενής, *constant.*

12. Ἐλαιῶνος, *Olivet;* for ἐλαιῶν, ἐλαιῶνος means *an*

olive-grove, in Latin *olivetum*, from which the name Olivet is given to the Mount, which stands on the eastern side of Jerusalem, the brook Kidron running in the valley between.

12. ἔχον should be rendered literally *having*. The classical expression is ἄπεχον, *being distant* (Thuc. viii. 67), followed by the accusative *of distance*. See also Thuc. viii. 138.

— σαββάτου ὁδόν, a *Sabbath-day's journey*, two thousand paces, or about six furlongs, reckoned from the wall of a city in which a man lived. The distance was that of the ark from the tents in the wilderness.

13. Four catalogues of the Apostles are given ; by St. Matthew, St. Mark, St. Luke in his Gospel, and here. As to ten names the lists agree.

The remaining two are thus supplied :—

St. Matthew.	*St. Mark.*	*St. Luke.*
Lebbæus called Thaddæus.	Thaddæus.	Judas (son) of James.
Simon Cananites.	Simon Cananites.	Simon Zelotes.

Perhaps Lebbæus and Thaddæus were surnames of Judas.

Certainly *Cananites* in Hebrew and *Zelotes* in Greek have the same meaning ; for *Cananites* is from a Syriac word applied to the Jewish faction called "the Zelotes". See Bp. Lightfoot on Gal. i. 14.

— Ἰούδας Ἰακώβου. Judas (son) of James. The rendering *brother of James* in the Auth. Ver. was suggested by Jude i. 1.

— προσκαρτεροῦντες, *strict in their attendance*. Participle of προσκαρτερέω, *to persist in* a thing, *to apply diligently to* it. Notice the use of εἶναι, especially in the *imperfect*, with the present participle, often with the simple sense of the finite verb, and sometimes to emphasize the predicate.

14. καὶ Μαρίᾳ, *especially Mary.* The Blessed Virgin is here distinguished from the rest of the women. It is the last mention of her in the New Testament.

15. ὀνομάτων, *persons. Names* put for *persons* by a Hebrew usage.

— ἐπὶ τὸ αὐτό, *at the same place.*

16. τοῖς συλλαβοῦσι, *to those who apprehended.*

17. κλῆρον, *lot,* that is, *an allotted portion.*

The earliest meaning of κλῆρος was *a lot* or *a counter* used in deciding a dispute. Thus in Homer we read of the Grecian chieftains each marking a κλῆρος, and then of all the κλῆροι being cast about in a helmet, the first which leaped out being the winning lot.

Subsequently κλῆρος was used for *a possession obtained by lot,* and hence for *an allotted portion or office,* as in this passage.

18. ἐκτήσατο, *purchased,* or, as some take it, *caused the purchase.*

The account given by St. Matthew of this matter contains two statements not quite in accordance with the description here given. He says—

(1) That the Chief Priests bought the field.

(2) That the field was called *The Field of Blood* because it was bought with the *price of blood.*

The usual solutions of these discrepancies are—

(a) Judas was the cause of the purchase of the field by the Priests.

(β) The field received its name for the reasons given by *both* of the Evangelists.

Observe, however, *the design* of each writer, and remember that both histories are *fragmentary.*

St. Matthew dwells more on the fulfilment of the *prophecy* relating to the Potter's Field (Zech. xi. 13).

St Luke has in view the base selfishness and horrible fate of the traitorous *Apostle.*

18. ἐλάκησε, *he burst asunder.* 1 aor. of λάσκω, *to break with a crash.*

The 2 aor. form λακεῖν occurs more frequently in Attic writers.

20. ἔπαυλις, *habitation.* Properly the hut in which the shepherd watches the fold.

21. ἐπισκοπήν, *office.* Literally, *the office of a watcher or guardian.*

— εἰσῆλθε καὶ ἐξῆλθεν ἐφ᾽ ἡμᾶς, *came in and went out among us,* is a brief way of expressing εἰσῆλθεν ἐφ᾽ ἡμᾶς καὶ ἐξῆλθεν ἀφ᾽ ἡμῶν.

22. τοῦ βαπτίσματος Ἰωάννου. Since it was from the time when our Lord was baptized by John that His *ministerial* capacity dated, a sign from heaven confirming His authority.

23. ἔστησαν. 1 aor. *they put forward.*

24. κύριε. The prayer was probably addressed to Christ.

— ἐξελέξω, *thou didst choose.*

25. παρέβη, *transgressed.*

26. κλήρους αὐτῶν, lots (*bearing the names) of them.*
But the true reading is αὐτοῖς, *for them* or *to them.*

CHAPTER II.

1. ἐν τῷ συμπληροῦσθαι τὴν ἡμέραν τῆς Πεντηκοστῆς, *while the day of Pentecost was being completed.* An accusative and infinitive clause is often used as a noun after the article.

— Πεντηκοστῆς. The Feast of Weeks, of Wheat-harvest, of First-fruits, was the second of the great festivals of the Hebrews. It was kept on the 50th day from the 2nd day of the Passover, and lasted one day. The distinguishing rite of the day was the offering of two loaves, the first that were made from the new wheat.

— ἐπὶ τὸ αὐτό, *at the same place.*

2. φερομένης, *rushing.* The passive of φέρω is frequently used of *rapid* motion.

— οἶκον, *apartment* or *chamber*, probably the *upper-room* of i. 15.

3. ὤφθησαν, *there appeared.*

— διαμεριζόμεναι, *distributing themselves* from one source.

— ἐκάθισε. Sc. γλῶσσα (*a tongue*), *settled.* The singular is used because of ἕνα ἕκαστον.

4. ἑτέραις, *other* than they had ever known.

— ἀποφθέγγεσθαι, *power of utterance.* The infinitive used as a noun.

5. εὐλαβεῖς, *devout.* The word in Attic Greek means *cautious, circumspect.*

— κατοικοῦντες, *residing :* some permanently, others only for the time of the feast.

6. φωνῆς probably means the *sound* of the *rushing mighty wind*.

— συνεχύθη, *was confounded*.

— ἤκουον εἶς ἔκαστος αὐτῶν, *they, every one (of them), heard them*.

7. ἐξίσταντο, *were astonished*.

8. ἡμεῖς ἀκούομεν ἔκαστος, *we hear (them), each (of us)*.

9. Ἐλαμῖται. Inhabitants of Elam, a district near the Persian Gulf.

— Μεσοποταμίαν. The district between the rivers Euphrates and Tigris.

— Ἀσίαν. By Asia in the New Testament we are to understand that part of Asia Minor which borders on the Ægæan Sea, including the provinces of Mysia, Lydia. and Caria, the chief city being Ephesus.

10. οἱ ἐπιδημοῦντες κ.τ.λ., *and sojourners from Rome, some of them Jews and some Proselytes*. Some of these visitors from Rome were Jews by *birth*, others by *conversion*.

— προσήλυτοι. The word, which in classical Greek means *new-comers*, was used for those *strangers* who in all stages of Jewish history held the faith and adopted the ritual of the Israelites. About the second century, if not earlier, these Proselytes were divided into two classes :

(1) Proselytes of the Gate, who were allowed to dwell within Jewish cities on condition of renouncing heathen superstitions and observing certain precepts of the Law of Moses.

(2) Proselytes of Righteousness, who, having been baptized and circumcised, were admitted to all

rites, ceremonies, and privileges used or enjoyed by natural Jews.

11. μεγαλεῖα. An adjective, *magnificent, wonderful.* Supply ἔργα.

12. διηποροῦντο, *were perplexed.*

— τί ἂν θέλοι τοῦτο εἶναι; *what can this be?* ἄν is frequently used with the optative in an interrogative sentence. Compare xvii. 18.

13. γλεύκους. Genitive of γλεῦκος, *sweet young wine.* Latin, *mustum.*

14. ἐνωτίσασθε, *give ear.* 1 aor. imperative ἐνωτίζομαι, from ἐν and ὦτα, *ears,* a word of late Greek.

15. ὥρα τρίτη. The third hour would be about eight o'clock at this season. The Jews at this time divided the day into twelve equal portions between sunrise and sunset. The fixed hours of prayer were the third, sixth, and ninth, and no pious Jew would eat or drink before the third hour.

17. ἐσχάταις ἡμέραις. By the *last days* we may understand the whole period between the first and second comings of the Messiah; the days of the Christian Dispensation.

18. ἐκχεῶ. The true form of this future is ἐκχέω.

20. ἐπιφανῆ, *glorious, notable.* Thuc. vi. 72.

22. ἀποδεδειγμένον, *accredited,* from ἀποδείκνυμι, *to make known, to demonstrate.*

Our Lord was proved to be what He claimed to be; He received from God (ἀπὸ τοῦ Θεοῦ) credentials of His claims.

— δυνάμεσι. Miracles are called by various names in Scripture, *e.g.*:

δυνάμεις, *mighty works*, as evidencing the *power* of God.

τέρατα, *marvels*, as proofs of *supernatural* agency.

σημεῖα, *signs*, as *evidences* of a divine *mission*.

23. ὡρισμένῃ, *determined*, from ὁρίζω, *to define, to determine*.

— ἔκδοτον, *delivered up*.

— διὰ χειρὸς ἀνόμων, *by the hand of lawless men*, by means of the Roman soldiers, who were not *under the law*. Notice διά with the *instrumental* cause, as in ii. 22.

The Roman soldiers were the *causa instrumentalis*, the Jews were the *causa principalis*.

— προσπήξαντες, *having nailed up*, i.e. to the cross.

— ἀνείλετε, *ye slew*.

24. ὠδῖνας, *pangs*. ὠδίς is used for *the pangs of childbirth* and, generally, for *pain, distress*.

But it is possible that the word is used here, as it is in the Septuagint, for *snares* or *bonds*.

— ὑπ' αὐτοῦ, *by it*, i.e. by death.

25. εἰς αὐτόν, *with reference to him*.

— προορώμην, *I saw before me*. The Attic imperfect middle of ὁράω is ἑωρώμην.

— σαλευθῶ, from σαλεύω, *I shake*.

26. εὐφράνθη, from εὐφραίνω, *I am glad*.

— ἠγαλλιάσατο, from ἀγαλλιάομαι, *I rejoice*.

— κατασκηνώσει ἐπ' ἐλπίδι, *shall pitch its tent on hope*.

27. εἰς ᾅδην, *within Hades*. *Hell* in its primary meaning signifies *the unseen and covered place*, and so is a correct rendering of ᾅδης, *the unseen place*, the invisible mansion of disembodied souls.

28. ἐγνώρισας, *thou didst make known.*

29. ἐξόν. Supply ἔστω, *let it be permitted.* ἐξόν is participle of the impersonal ἔξεστι. The Revised Version supplies ἐστί, with which the meaning is *it is permitted.*

— πατριάρχου. *Patriarch* here means head of (the royal) family.

— ἐν ἡμῖν, *in the midst of us,* the tomb of the royal family being *in* Jerusalem.

30. καθίσαι, *to cause (one) to sit.*

31. προϊδών, *having looked into futurity.*

32. οὗ, *of whom,* or, more probably, *of which fact.*

33. τῇ δεξιᾷ, probably not *local, at his right hand,* but *instrumental, by his right hand,* i.e. by his power.

34. λέγει δὲ αὐτός, *and yet he says.*

36. πᾶς οἶκος Ἰσραήλ. The article is omitted after πᾶς because οἶκος Ἰσραήλ is treated as a proper name.

37. κατενύγησαν, *they were pricked.* 2 aor. pass. κατα-νύττω, *compungo.*

38. ἐπί, *in reliance upon.*

39. εἰς μακράν, *afar off,* either *in distance* or *in time.*

40. διεμαρτύρατο, *he solemnly testified.* 1 aor. διαμαρ-τύρομαι. Observe the force of the preposition. Another reading is the imperfect διεμαρτύρετο.

— σώθητε, *be saved,* i.e. by God; or the passive may be put in a middle sense, *save yourselves,* which is a common usage in this late Greek.

— σκολιᾶς, *crooked* or *perverse.*

41. προσετέθησαν, *were added.*

42. προσκαρτεροῦντες, *constant in their attendance.*

This verse is deemed of great importance, since from it we seem to gather a summary of the state of society in the early Church. The members attended to the teaching of the Apostles, partook of the Common Meal (probably not the Holy Eucharist), and joined in the Common Prayers. The articles prefixed to all the substantives lead us to conclude that *regular* customs are described.

43. ἐγένετο, *fell.* Aorist.

— ἐγίνετο, *were continually wrought.* Imperfect.

44. ἐπὶ τὸ αὐτό, *at the same place.*

45. κτήματα, *lands,* used for things that *cannot be moved.*

— ὑπάρξεις, *goods, chattels,* used for things that *can be moved.* In classical Greek ἔπιπλα, *things that lie on the surface,* not fixed or rooted, as are lands, houses, trees.

46. κατ᾿ οἶκον, *in private houses,* opposed to ἐν τῷ ἱερῷ. They prayed in the Temple, they took their meals in private dwellings.

— ἀγαλλιάσει, *gladness.*

— ἀφελότητι, *singleness, simplicity.* From ἀφελής, *without stones* (φελλεύς meaning *stony ground*), and hence *level, plain.*

47. προσετίθει, *kept adding.* Imperfect.

— τοὺς σωζομένους, *those who were in the way of salvation; those who accepted the offer of salvation.* The *present* participle seems to require this rendering.

CHAPTER III.

1. ἐπὶ τὸ αὐτὸ, *at the same place.*

— τὴν ἐννάτην. The ninth hour, at the season of the year when day and night are of equal length, would correspond to our 3 P.M.

2. ὑπάρχων, *being.* Observe that ὑπάρχω is sometimes used for εἰμί in the Acts, as for instance in iii. 9 ; iv. 34. The verbs ὑπάρχειν, εἶναι, γίγνεσθαι stand to one another in the relation of past, present, and future ; to be already in existence, to be, and to become. Cope on Arist. Rhet. A. 4, 19.

— ἐβαστάζετο, *was being carried.*

— ἐτίθουν, *they were in the habit of placing.*

— ὡραίαν, *beautiful.* This was probably a gate leading from the Court of the Gentiles into the Court of the Women, opposite the cloisters mentioned in verse 11.

— τοῦ αἰτεῖν, *for the purpose of asking.* Genitive of *design.* The infinitive with the genitive of the article is sometimes used in Attic to express cause, design, or motive, as in Thuc. i. 4, and ii. 32.

— τοὺς εἰσπορευομένους, *whoever entered ;* not those then entering or about to enter.

5. ἐπεῖχεν, *fixed his attention.* τὸν νοῦν may be supplied.

6. οὐχ ὑπάρχει, *are not.*

7. πιάσας, *having taken hold.* From πιάζω, a Doric form of πιέζω, *I press.*

— αἱ βάσεις, *the soles of his feet.*

7. τὰ σφυρά, *his ankle-joints.*

8. ἐξαλλόμενος, *springing-up.*

10. ἐπεγίνωσκον, *they began to recognise.*

— θάμβους, *awe.*

— ἐκστάσεως, *amazement.*

11. κρατοῦντος κ.τ.λ., *when the lame man who was healed was keeping fast hold.* Observe the genitive absolute, which generally defines the *time* of an action.

— συνέδραμε, *ran together.*

— ἐπὶ τῇ στοᾷ, *at the porch.* This porch, by which we may understand *cloisters,* was on the eastern side of Herod's Temple. Josephus says it was a part of Solomon's Temple that had been preserved, but it seems more probable that Herod built it, and that it was merely named after Solomon.

— ἔκθαμβοι, *awe-struck.*

12. ἐπὶ τούτῳ, *at this man* or *over this man.*

— ὡς πεποιηκόσι, *as having caused,* i.e. *as if we had caused.* ὡς is often prefixed to a participle to express a ground of belief or a cause of action.

— τοῦ περιπατεῖν, *to walk.* The use of the infinitive with the genitive of the article to express *design* (see iii. 2) was so common in later Greek, that the construction was often employed in a loose manner after verbs of *causing,* or any words *implying design.*

13. παῖδα, probably here *servant;* υἱός being commonly used when Christ is called *the Son.*

— παρεδώκατε, *gave up,* i.e. to the Roman government.

— ἠρνήσασθε, *ye denied.*

— ἀπολύειν, *to set (Him) free.*

14. χαρισθῆναι. From χαρίζομαι, I make a free gift.

15. οὗ, of whom, or more probably of which fact, i.e. of the Resurrection.

16. ἐπὶ τῇ πίστει, in reliance on faith.

— τὸ ὄνομα αὐτοῦ, His Name. Observe that the Apostles performed miracles in and in a manner by the Name of Jesus.

— ἡ δι' αὐτοῦ, that comes through Him.

— ὁλοκληρίαν, perfect soundness. From ὁλόκληρος, quite sound.

18. After ὁ δὲ Θεός take ἐπλήρωσεν οὕτως.

19. ἐξαλειφθῆναι. 1 aor. inf. pass. ἐξαλείφω, I blot out.

— ὅπως ἄν, so that. ἄν is sometimes joined to ὡς and ὅπως before the subjunctive in a final clause without adding any force that can be made perceptible in English.

— ἀναψύξεως, of refreshment. ἀνάψυξις is a word of late Greek, from ἀναψύχω, I revive with fresh air, I refresh. By the seasons of refreshment we may perhaps understand the period of the Messiah's Second Advent.

20. προκεχειρισμένον, appointed.

21. δέξασθαι, contain.

— ἀποκαταστάσεως, of the restoration.

— ἀπ' αἰῶνος, from time immemorial. αἰών is used for an indefinite period of time.

22. ἀκούσεσθε, ye shall hear. Observe the future.

23. ἐξολοθρευθήσεται, shall be completely destroyed.

24. τῶν καθεξῆς (ὄντων), those who followed in regular succession.

καθεξῆς is an adverb equivalent to the more common ἐφεξῆς.

25. διέθετο, *covenanted.*

— πατριαί, *families.*

26. παῖδα, *servant.* See note on verse 13.

— ἐν τῷ ἀποστρέφειν, *in turning away.* ἐν denotes *the sphere in which* the saving power of Christ is displayed.

CHAPTER IV.

1. ἐπέστησαν, *came suddenly upon them.* A classical use of the word. See Thuc. viii. 69.

— ὁ στρατηγὸς τοῦ ἱεροῦ, *the commander of the Temple-(guard).* The commander of the armed guard of Levites on duty in the Temple.

2. διαπονούμενοι, *being disturbed.*

— ἐν τῷ 'Ιησοῦ, *in Jesus;* the Resurrection of our Lord being the *foundation* of the doctrine of the resurrection from the dead.

3. εἰς τήρησιν, *into ward.*

4. ἐγενήθην was a Doric form equivalent to the Attic ἐγενόμην.

5. αὐτῶν, *of the Jews.*

— ἄρχοντας, *rulers;* here used probably for the *chief-priests,* ἀρχιερεῖς, the heads of the twenty-four sacerdotal families.

— πρεσβυτέρους, *elders;* men of advanced age, famed for wisdom and piety.

2

5. γραμματεῖς, *scribes;* the recognised expounders of
the Law.

These *three classes* composed the Sanhedrin or Supreme
Court of Justice, with seventy-two members.

6. Annas had been deposed from the office of High-
priest by the Roman government, and Caiaphas, his
son-in-law, was at this time High-priest. Still as we find
both of these persons mentioned as possessors of the
office (even at the same time in Luke iii. 2), we may
suppose that the Jews regarded Annas as the legitimate
High-priest, while Caiaphas was recognised as such by
the Roman government.

7. ἐν τῷ μέσῳ. The Sanhedrin sat in the form of a
semicircle.

— ἐποιήσατε, *did.* The aorist marks a single act.

— ὑμεῖς. Emphatic ; common folk like you.

9. ἀνακρινόμεθα, *are being examined.* See xii. 19.

— ἐπὶ εὐεργεσίᾳ ἀνθρώπου ἀσθενοῦς, *with respect to the
good service done to the sick man.*

— ἐν τίνι, *by what means.*

— σέσωσται, *has been cured.*

10. ἐν τούτῳ, *by this (Name).*

11. ἐξουθενηθείς, *set at naught.* From ἐξουθενέω, a
word of late Greek.

12. ἡ σωτηρία, *the expected salvation.* Observe the
force of the article.

13. παρρησίαν, *boldness of speech.* From πᾶν and ῥῆμα.

— ἰδιῶται, *ignorant;* always used of men ignorant of
the particular matter under discussion (Thuc. vi. 72).
So here it means " unskilled in *religious* knowledge ".

— ἐπεγίνωσκον, *they began to recognise.*

15. συνέβαλον, *they conferred.*

17. διανεμηθῇ, *should be spread abroad.*

— ἀπειλῇ ἀπειλησώμεθα, *let us threaten with a threat,* i.e. *let us straitly threaten.* Some editors omit ἀπειλῇ. The cognate dative is used in place of an adverb to express *intenseness.* See v. 28, and xxiii. 14.

18. καθόλου, *absolutely.*

20. εἴδομεν, *we saw.*

21. προσαπειλησάμενοι, *having added more threats.*

— τὸ πῶς κολάσωνται, *whereby they might punish.* The article prefixed to the clause calls especial attention to the fact that they had no ground of accusation. The whole clause πῶς κολάσωνται αὐτούς stands as a noun attached to the article.

22. ἐτῶν γάρ. The man's age is noticed to show that his person and malady were well known to the people.

24. ὁ ποιήσας, *who didst make.*

25. ἐφρύαξαν ἔθνη, *did the Gentiles rage.* φρυάσσω =*ferocio,* is only found in the middle in classical Greek, strictly of spirited horses, *to neigh,* and hence *to be insolent.*

26. παρέστησαν, *stood side by side ;* as if in battle-array against the Lord.

— ἐπὶ τὸ αὐτό, *at the same place.*

27. ἔχρισας, *Thou didst anoint.*

— τε, *namely.* They specify Herod as the representative of οἱ βασιλεῖς, and Pontius Pilate of οἱ ἄρχοντες in verse 26.

28. λαοῖς, *peoples, i.e. tribes.* Keep the plural.

— προώρισε, *determined beforehand.*

29. τανῦν, *at this present time.*

— ἔπιδε, *keep watch, i.e.* so as to frustrate them.

30. ἐν τῷ ἐκτείνειν σε, *while thou art stretching forth.* An infinitive clause is often governed by a preposition; in which case the article is always prefixed to the clause. Here the clause expresses the dative of *manner.*

31. δεηθέντων αὐτῶν, *when they had prayed.*

32. πλήθους, *main body* of the believers.

— οὐδὲ εἷς, *not even one.*

— τῶν ὑπαρχόντων αὐτῷ, *of the things belonging to him.*

— ἴδιον, *his own* private and peculiar property.

33. ἀπεδίδουν, *rendered.* The word implies that they *gave* of what they had *received.* They held the testimony of the Resurrection as *a trust* for the benefit of all.

— ἀποδιδόναι is (1) to give back, (2) to render as a *due,* (3) to fulfil duly any office or duty, as ἀποδιδόναι λόγον, *to render an account,* Acts xix. 40, and so to explain or set forth any statement or doctrine. Cope on Arist. Rhet. A. 1, 7. See also Thuc. ii. 71.

— χάρις, *grace* from God.

34. ἐνδεής, *in poverty, in absolute want.*

35. διεδίδοτο, used impersonally, *distribution was made.*

36. παρακλήσεως. Barnabas gained his name probably from possessing an extraordinary gift of *exhortation,* which is indeed mentioned as a characteristic of that Apostle in xi. 23. Being born in Cyprus he may

have been acquainted with St. Paul (since Tarsus was within sight of Cyprus) in early life. He introduced St. Paul to the Church at Jerusalem (ix. 27).

— Λευίτης. The Levites were allowed, after the Captivities, to possess estates in Palestine.

Jeremiah, a Levite, bought a field (Jer. xxxii. 7).

37. τὸ χρῆμα, *the money* paid for it.

CHAPTER V.

1. Ananias and Sapphira desired to gain the credit of holy zeal without parting with self-advantage. They professed to give the *whole* price, while they kept back a portion. They wished to serve *two* masters while they seemed to be serving only *one*.

— κτῆμα, *a piece of land.*

— ἐνοσφίσατο, *kept back, put on one side* part of the price.

2. συνειδυίας, *being conscious of it.* Participle of σύνοιδα.

3. ἐπλήρωσεν. Satan not only suggested the sin, but *gained full possession* of the heart of the sinner, to the exclusion of the Holy Spirit.

— ψεύσασθαί σε, *that you lied to.*

4. μένον, *while it remained.* Neut. part. of μένω.

— οὐχί σοι ἔμενε ; *was it not remaining in thy possession ?*

— καὶ πραθὲν (οὐχὶ) ὑπῆρχε ; *and when sold was it* (*not*) ?

4. τί (ἐστιν) ὅτι ἔθου ; *why is it that thou didst put?*

— ἐψεύσω, *thou didst lie.*

— ἀνθρώποις. The *dative* after ψεύδομαι implies *injury* or *insult.*

5. ἐξέψυξε is a word of late Greek.   In Thuc. i. 134 ἀποψύχω is used.

6. οἱ νεώτεροι, *the younger men.* Some have considered that these were a distinct *class* as opposed to οἱ πρεσβύτεροι : but this seems unnecessary.

— συνέστειλαν, *wrapped up* in grave-clothes, or in his garments.

7. διάστημα, *an interval.*

8. εἰ ἀπέδοσθε ; *did ye sell ?*   See note on i. 6.
ἀποδίδωμι, *I give back;* ἀποδίδομαι, *I sell;* fut. ἀποδώσομαι, *I will sell;* 2 aor. ἀπεδόμην, *I sold.*

9. τί (ἐστιν) ὅτι ; *why is it that ?*

— συνεφωνήθη ὑμῖν, *an agreement was made between you.*

— πειράσαι, *to tempt* or *to try.*

11. ἐκκλησία means properly, *the general assembly of persons called out* (ἐκκαλέω) *from among others for a particular purpose.*   Hence in the New Testament it bears these meanings :

    (1) An assembly (Acts xix. 41).

    (2) The society of Christ's followers (Acts ii. 47).

    (3) The society of Christians in a particular *district* (Acts xiii. 1).

    (4) The society of Christians in a single *family* (Rom. xvi. 5).

13. τῶν λοιπῶν, *of the rest*, referring perhaps to the rulers, as opposed to ὁ λαός.

— κολλᾶσθαι, *to associate himself.*

14. μᾶλλον, *yet more than before*, referring to iv. 4.

— τῷ κυρίῳ depends on προσετίθεντο, as in xi. 24.

15. πλατείας (ὁδούς), *broad-ways, streets.*

— κραβάττων, *couches.* In Latin, *grabātus is a pallet-bed.*

— κἄν = καὶ ἐάν, *at the least.*

— ἵνα ἐπισκευάσει. The future indicative is put instead of the subjunctive for vividness. See note on xxi. 24.

16. συνήρχετο εἰς, *came together to Jerusalem.* Notice the preposition.

— ὀχλουμένους, *troubled.*

17. οἱ σὺν αὐτῷ, *his companions, his party.*

— αἵρεσις, *party.* The word signified (1) *a choice*, (2) *a party*, (3) *a division* in Church matters (1 Cor. xi. 19), (4) *the open espousal of any fundamental error.*

— ζῆλου, *indignation.*

20. τῆς ζωῆς ταύτης, *of this life.* *Life* is put for *Christian doctrine.* The force of ταύτης is *which we are engaged in preaching.*

21. ὑπὸ τὸν ὄρθρον, *towards daybreak.*

— τὸ συνέδριον, *the Sanhedrin.*

— τὴν γερουσίαν, *the Senate.*

— ἀχθῆναι αὐτούς, *that they should be brought.*

22. οἱ ὑπηρέται, *the servants.*

24. ὁ στρατηγὸς τοῦ ἱεροῦ. See note on iv. 1.

— διηπόρουν, *they were in doubt.*

26. λιθασθῶσιν, *they should be stoned.*

28. οὐ παραγγελίᾳ παρηγγείλαμεν; *did we not charge with an injunction?* See iv. 17.

— ἐπί, *with reference to,* or *in reliance upon.*

30. διεχειρίσασθε, *slew.* διαχειρίζομαι has this meaning in late Greek.

— ἐπὶ ξύλου, *on a tree.* This word for the Cross is peculiar to St. Luke and St. Paul. Compare Gal. iii. 13 with Deut. xxi. 23.

31. τῇ δεξιᾷ αὐτοῦ, *by his right hand,* i.e. by his power.

32. ῥημάτων, *statements,* usually statements *of facts.*

— καὶ τὸ Πνεῦμα δὲ τὸ "Αγιον, *and so also is, on the other hand, the Holy Spirit.* Observe the force of δέ. The Apostles bore witness *externally,* the Holy Spirit *internally.*

33. διεπρίοντο, *were cut asunder* (*in their hearts*). See vii. 54.

— ἐβουλεύοντο, *took counsel.*

— ἀνελεῖν, *to kill.*

34. Gamaliel was a Rabbi of great repute. He was the teacher of St. Paul.

— βραχύ τι, *some short time.*

— ποιῆσαι, *to put.*

36. Θευδᾶς. Josephus mentions a great revolt under one Theudas about A.D. 44, i.e. 12 years *later* than this speech. Again, Josephus places the revolt of Judas the Galilæan in A.D. 8, where St. Luke places it, i.e. about 24 years *before* this speech. Hence, if the writer has made an error, it is an error of 12 + 24 or 36 years,

since he places Theudas *before* Judas; and as this is quite inconsistent with St. Luke's usual accuracy, we conclude that *his* Theudas is not the Theudas of Josephus.

36. τινα, *some important person.*

— προσεκολλήθη, *joined themselves;* but the true reading is προσεκλίθη, with the same meaning in late Greek.

— ἀνῃρέθη, *was killed.*

— διελύθησαν, *were broken up.*

37. τῆς ἀπογραφῆς, *of the making of the census-roll,* when Quirinus was Governor of Syria. Comp. Luke ii. 2.

— ἀπέστησε, *led away.*

— διεσκορπίσθησαν, *were scattered abroad.*

39. μήποτε, *lest haply, ne forte.*

41. ὑπὲρ τοῦ ὀνόματος, *in behalf of the Name.* The best MSS. omit αὐτοῦ.

42. πᾶσαν ἡμέραν, *every day.*

— κατ᾽ οἶκον, *at home, in the house.*

— τὸν Χριστὸν Ἰησοῦν, *Jesus as the Christ.*

CHAPTER VI.

1. πληθυνόντων, *increasing in number.* Here in a *neuter* sense.

— τῶν Ἑλληνιστῶν, *the Hellenists,* used in the New Testament for those Jews who lived in foreign countries, spoke the Greek language, and used the Septuagint Version of the Scriptures.

1. τοὺς Ἐβραίους, *the Hebrews*, the Jews of Palestine, who spoke the Syro-Chaldaic language, and used the Hebrew Scriptures.

— παρεθεωροῦντο, *were overlooked, were passed by with contempt*.

2. τὸ πλῆθος, *the main body*.

— οὐκ ἀρεστόν ἐστιν, *it is not an agreeable thing, it seems not desirable*.

— καταλείψαντας. The aorist ἔλειψα is not classical, ἔλιπον being always used: the author of the Acts uses κατέλιπον in all other passages, xviii. 19, xxi. 3, xxiv. 27.

— τραπέζαις, *tables*, at which the daily food was distributed.

3. μαρτυρουμένους, *well spoken of, of good report*.

— μαρτύρομαι = *I testify;* μαρτυροῦμαι = *I am testified of*.

— χρείας, *service*.

4. προσκαρτερήσομεν, *will give constant attention*.

5. ἤρεσεν ὁ λόγος, *the proposal found favour*.

The names of the Seven Deacons are all of *Greek* derivation, whence it is concluded that they were chosen from the Hellenistic part of the community. The original office of these ministers was that of "Almoners," but it is clear from the subsequent histories of Stephen and Philip that they were not debarred from baptizing and preaching. The functions of Deacons increased in importance as the need and the resources of the Church increased.

— Φίλιππον. Philip preached in Samaria, viii. 5;

converted the Eunuch, viii. 26 ; and had four daughters who had the gift of prophecy, xxi. 8.

6. ἐπέθηκαν χεῖρας. This is the first mention in the New Testament of the imposition of hands as a symbol of ordination. The form was prescribed to Moses as the sign of conveying authority to Joshua.

7. πολύς τε ὄχλος τῶν ἱερέων. The number of priests at Jerusalem was very large ; according to Josephus, 20,000. The priests who came back from Babylon were in number 4289.

8. ἐποίει, was continually working.

9. συναγωγῆς. There were 480 Synagogues in Jerusalem at that time.

— Λιβερτίνων. From the Latin libertini, freedmen. These were probably descendants of Jews who, having been taken in war and made slaves at Rome, had regained their freedom. These Libertini may have returned to Jerusalem of their own will, or in consequence of a decree of Tiberius that all Jews should leave Italy.

τῶν . . . τῶν. Two Synagogue-corporations are specified, one composed of the Libertini, the people of Cyrene (a city in Africa on the northern coast) and Alexandria ; the other of the natives of Cilicia and Asia.

— συζητοῦντες, disputing. The word properly means making a joint enquiry.

11. ὑπέβαλον, they suborned, literally they put forward in an underhand manner. In classical Greek the middle is used (1) for substituting another's child for one's own ; (2) for bringing false accusations.

12. ἐπιστάντες, *coming suddenly (upon him).*

13. τούτου. Pointing to the Temple, *yonder Holy Place*, or *this Holy Place*, if we suppose the Sanhedrin to be then sitting in a room of the Temple.

14. ἀλλάξει, *shall alter*, or perhaps stronger, *shall abrogate* (Heb. i. 12).

— πρόσωπον ἀγγέλου. Probably a supernatural brightness, like that which rested on the face of Moses when he came down from Sinai.

CHAPTER VII.

1. Stephen had been accused of proclaiming Jesus Christ as the destroyer of the Temple and the Law, and we have in this chapter the *commencement* of his defence. He traces the manifestations of God's favour to the Israelites from the call of Abraham to the building of the Temple, and thus proves that God was ever present with His chosen people, and that it was only from His *Presence* that the Temple derived its dignity. Had he not been interrupted in his speech, it seems probable that he would have asserted that this *Visible Presence of God* had been transferred from the Holy of Holies to the Body of Christ.

— εἰ ἄρα; *is it possible that?* ἄρα gives emphasis to the question.

2. ὁ Θεὸς τῆς δόξης, *the God of the Glory*; δόξα referring to the Visible Presence of God, the Shechinah.

— πρὶν ἢ κατοικῆσαι αὐτόν, *before he dwelt.* 1 aor.

κατοικέω. πρὶν ἤ, like πρίν, may be followed by the infinitive, but πρότερον ἤ is more usual in Attic.

2. Χαῤῥάν, *Haran* in the Old Testament, in the south of Mesopotamia, famous as the scene of the defeat of Crassus by the Parthians. Comp. Lucan i. 104.

miserando funere Crassus
Assyrias Latio maculavit sanguine Carras.

3. δεῦρο, *come hither.*

4. μετὰ τὸ ἀποθανεῖν τὸν πατέρα. It appears from the chronology that Terah lived sixty years *after* Abraham left him. But Stephen quotes the facts in the order in which they are placed in Genesis xi. 32, and xii. 1, and neglects the order in which they occurred.

— κατῴκησεν, *he dwelt.* 1 aor. κατοικέω.

— μετῴκισεν, (*God*) *removed him.* Observe the change of subject. 1 aor. μετοικίζω.

5. βῆμα ποδός, *standing-ground for his foot.*

— εἰς κατάσχεσιν, *for a possession.* See verse 45.

6. πάροικον, *sojourning.*

— δουλώσουσιν αὐτό, (*the foreigners*) *shall make slaves of it.*

— τετρακόσια. From the going of Abraham into Egypt to the Exodus were 430 years. But Stephen quotes the exact words of Gen. xv. 13.

7. ᾧ ἂν δουλεύσωσι, *to which they shall be in bondage.* Some read the fut. indic. δουλεύσουσι.

N.B.—δουλεύω, *I am a slave.*
   δουλόω, *I make a slave of another.*

7. τόπῳ τούτῳ. From Exod. iii. 12, *ye shall serve God on this mountain*.

8. οὕτως, *thus*, *i.e.* under the covenant ratified by circumcision.

9. ἀπέδοντο, *sold*. See v. 8.

— ἦν ὁ Θεὸς μετ᾽ αὐτοῦ. These are important words. God's favour was with Joseph *in Egypt*, and was not confined to *the land of Canaan*.

10. ἐξείλατο, *rescued*.

— κατέστησεν, (*Pharaoh*) *made*. Observe the change of subject.

11. χορτάσματα, *provender ;* strictly food for *cattle*.

12. σῖτα, *corn*. Observe that σῖτος masc. has a neut. plural σῖτα.

13. ἀνεγνωρίσθη, *was recognised*.

14. μετεκαλέσατο, *invited to dwell with him*.

— ἐν ψυχαῖς ἑβδομήκοντα πέντε, *consisting of seventy-five persons*. συνισταμένην may be supplied. The Hebrew of Gen. xlvi. 27 has *seventy*, but the Septuagint has *seventy-five*, including probably the children of Ephraim and Manasseh.

16. μετετέθησαν, *they were removed*.

— ἐτέθησαν, *were placed*.

The difficulties in this verse may be thus stated :

(a) Jacob was not buried at Shechem, but at Machpelah.

(β) Jacob, and not Abraham, bought a field in Shechem.

From Genesis we learn that Abraham bought Machpelah from the sons of Heth, and Jacob bought the field in Shechem from "the children of Hamor, Shechem's father"; also that Jacob was buried at Machpelah, and Joseph at Shechem.

These circumstances are apparently confused in Stephen's summary of the history of the Patriarchs.

16. τιμῆς ἀργυρίου. The price paid for *Machpelah* was four hundred shekels of silver.

— Ἐμμὸρ τοῦ Συχέμ, *Emmor (the father) of Sychem*, but the ellipsis of πατρός is uncommon, and for τοῦ some read ἐν.

17. ἦς, *which*, by attraction for ἥν.

— ὤμοσεν, *made with an oath*, but the better reading is ὡμολόγησεν, *made with a covenant*.

18. καθώς, *in proportion as*.

— ἄχρις οὗ, *until the time when*.

19. κατασοφισάμενος, *having dealt in a wily manner*. From Exod. i. 10.

— τοῦ ποιεῖν ἔκθετα, *so that they exposed*, or *so that he caused to be exposed*. The genitive of the infinitive is loosely used to express the *result* (see iii. 12) of the king's cruelty. Observe that ποιεῖν ἔκθετα = ἐκτίθεναι.

— εἰς τὸ μὴ ζωογονεῖσθαι, *in order that they should not be brought up alive*.

20. καιρῷ, *season*, i.e. opportune or critical. See i. 7.

— ἀστεῖος, *beautiful*. From ἄστυ, just as *urbanus* from *urbs*. The word is taken from the Sept. of Exod. ii. 2, *she saw he was a goodly child*. In classical Greek the word usually means *witty, polished*, with a reference to *language*.

— τῷ Θεῷ. Probably the dative of *opinion, before*

God, in the sight of God; implying that Moses was *very fair:* or it may be the *instrumental* dative, *by the aid of,* or *by the blessing of God.* Some take it for a Hebraism = *divinely, marvellously.*

20. ἀνετράφη, *was brought up.*

21. αὐτόν . . . αὐτόν. This repetition of the pronoun is probably for the sake of clearness, with some emphasis.

— ἐκτεθέντα, *exposed.*

— ἀνείλετο, *rescued.*

22. πάσῃ σοφίᾳ. Dative to denote *the means* of training.

— δυνατὸς ἐν λόγοις. This seems to contradict Exod. iv. 10, *I am not eloquent . . . I am slow of speech.* Some take λόγοις in the sense of *deliberations,* others refer it to *the writings* of Moses.

23. ἐπληροῦτο, *was being accomplished,* imperfect.

24. τῷ καταπονουμένῳ, *for him who was ill-treated.*

— πατάξας, *having smitten* violently, so as to cause his death.

25. δίδωσιν, *giveth,* or *was then giving;* the present is used to show that the work of liberation was just begun by the death of the Egyptian. The use of the present indicative gives vividness to the narration. See note on viii. 14.

26. ὤφθη, *he appeared, he showed himself;* the aorist expresses *suddenness.*

— συνήλασεν, *he brought together;* the aorist expresses that the act was *complete* on the part of Moses, though the men would not accept the reconciliation. But some read the imperfect συνήλλασσεν, "he tried to set them at one again".

27. ἀπώσατο, *thrust away.*

29. ἐν, *at,* or *in consequence of;* expressing the *ground* on which he fled.

— υἱούς. Their names were Gershom and Eliezer.

30. πληρωθέντων, *having been accomplished.*

— Σινᾶ. In Exodus *Horeb;* but they were parts of the same mountain-range.

— βάτου, *of a bush, i.e.* proceeding from a bush.

31. κατανοῆσαι, *to investigate it.*

33. ἅγια. Made *holy* by the *Presence* of the Divine Glory. See note on verse 2.

34. ἰδὼν εἶδον = *I have surely seen,* a Hebraism.

— ἀποστελῶ, *I will send;* but the true reading is ἀποστείλω, 1 aor. subj. *I would send.*

35. ἐν χειρί, *with the hand, i.e.* aided by the might.

36. ἐρυθρᾷ θαλάσσῃ. The Red Sea was so called from the colour of the seaweed on its shores. The name was applied by the Greeks to the Indian Ocean, the Persian and Arabian Gulfs. But the waters crossed by the Israelites were in the narrow creek running from the Arabian Gulf to the Isthmus of Suez.

37. ἀκούσεσθε, *ye shall hear.* Observe the *future.*

38. ἐν τῇ ἐκκλησίᾳ, *amid the assembly,* or *amid the congregation.*

— καὶ (μετὰ) τῶν πατέρων ἡμῶν, *and with our fathers.*

— λόγια, *oracles.* The word is used of the Old Testament Scriptures in Rom. iii. 2.

3

39. εἰς Αἴγυπτον, *to Egypt, i.e.* to the idol-worship of the Egyptians.

40. ὁ γὰρ Μωϋσῆς οὗτος. A nominative *without a verb*. Render it thus : " For this Moses, who brought us up out of the land of Egypt—we know not what has happened to him ".

41. ἐμοσχοποίησαν, *they made a calf.* The word occurs nowhere else.

42. ἔστρεψε, *turned away, i.e.* took no further thought about them. In xv. 16, we find ἀναστρέψω with the opposite meaning.

— τῇ στρατιᾷ τοῦ οὐράνου. The Sun, Moon, and Stars.

— βίβλῳ τῶν προφητῶν. The twelve Minor Prophets were included in one book.

— μὴ προσηνέγκατε; *did ye offer ?* The sense of the passage is this : " Ye surely cannot say that ye offered the sacrifices to *Me*, when ye were paying such honours to false gods ".

43. καὶ ἀνελάβετε, *and yet he uplifted, i.e.* carried about with pomp.

— Moloch, meaning *King*, was a deity worshipped by the Ammonites. Children were sacrificed to this idol, which was represented with the head of an ox.

— Remphan, in the Hebrew Chiun, supposed to be the same as Saturn, *a star* being his symbol.

— καὶ μετοικιῶ, *and therefore I will remove.* Att. fut. μετοικίζω.

— ἐπέκεινα. Adverb, for ἐπ' ἐκεῖνα, *on yonder side, beyond.* See Thuc. vi. 63.

43. Βαβυλῶνος. In the original, Amos v. 27, *Damascus.* Amos had the *Syrian* wars in view ; Stephen had the *Assyrian* captivities in his mind.

44. ἡ σκηνὴ τοῦ μαρτυρίου, *the Tabernacle of the Testimony*, *i.e.* the Ark, which contained the testimony of God written on the tables of stone. The *Presence* of God *on* the Ark, and His commandments *in* the Ark, kept up a perpetual *remembrance* of His Power.

— ἐν τοῖς πατράσιν ἡμῶν, *in the midst of our fathers.*

45. ἥν, *which (tabernacle).*

— εἰσήγαγον, *brought in* to Canaan.

— διαδεξάμενοι, *having received it in succession ;* the word used for the transmission of heirlooms.

— Ἰησοῦ, *Joshua*, the same name as Jesus.

— ἐν τῇ κατασχέσει, *while they were obtaining possession* of the land of the nations.

— ὧν by attraction for ἅ.

The names of the nations were Canaanites, Hittites, Hivites, Perizzites, Girgashites, Amorites, and Jebusites.

48. ὁ προφήτης. Isaiah lxvi. 1.

49. ὑποπόδιον τῶν ποδῶν μου, *the footstool of My feet.*

— καταπαύσεως, *final rest*, ἀντιπίπετετε, *resist.* Literally *rush against ; in adversum ruitis.*

52. τοῦ δικαίου, *of the Just One.* A regular title of the Messiah.

53. οἵτινες, *seeing that ye, quippe qui.* See ix. 35.

— εἰς διαταγὰς ἀγγέλων,. *as the ordinance of angels ;* literally, *unto ordinances of angels.* It implies that Angels assisted at the delivery of the Law.

54. διεπρίοντο, *they were cut asunder*. Literally *they were sawn asunder*.

55. ἑστῶτα, *standing;* the attitude of one ready to help.

56. τὸν υἱὸν τοῦ ἀνθρώπου. This title is only used *by Christ* of Himself in the Gospels.

58. ἔξω τῆς πόλεως. In accordance with the direction that criminals were to be stoned *without the camp* (Levit. xxiv. 14).

59. ἐπικαλούμενον, *making invocation*.

60. μὴ στήσῃς αὐτοῖς, *do not attach to them,* i.e. do not make this sin cleave to them. But some take στήσῃς in the sense of *weighing,* which is found in classical Greek, and explain it thus : *do not place in the scale of their offences.*

CHAPTER VIII.

1. συνευδοκῶν, *consenting*. The word occurs in Luke xi. 48 and Rom. i. 32, and in the three passages it implies that a greater degree of guilt is incurred by men who in cold blood sanction crimes, than by those who commit the crimes in the heat of passion.

— ἀναιρέσει, *destruction, slaying*.

— πάντες, *all the members,* i.e. τῆς ἐκκλησίας.

— διεσπάρησαν, *were scattered about*.

2. συνεκόμισαν, *buried*. συγκομίζω has these meanings :

(1) "I collect in a heap" the fruits of harvest.

(2) "I collect" the dead bodies from a field of battle, for burial. Thuc. vi. 71.

(3) "I assist in carrying out for burial" a single corpse. Soph. Aj. 1048.

2. κοπετόν, *lamentation*, accompanied by *beating* of the breast (κόπτομαι).

3. ἐλυμαίνετο, *went on making havoc of.* From λυμαίνω, *I maltreat.*

— κατὰ τοὺς οἴκους, *house after house.*

— σύρων, *dragging with violence.* The word implies *unnecessary violence.*

5. Philip the Deacon. See note on vi. 5.

— τὴν πόλιν, *the city* of Samaria.

— αὐτοῖς, *to the inhabitants.*

6. προσεῖχον (τὸν νοῦν), *paid attention.* See Thuc. vi. 93 and Dem. F. L. 58.

— ἐν τῷ ἀκούειν. The infinitive used as a substantive. See note on ii. 1.

7. Render *for many of those who had unclean spirits that cried with a loud voice came forth.* The construction is confused : to make it clear πολλοί has been changed to πολλῶν.

8. χαρά, *joy.* Distinguish it from χάρις, *grace.*

9. Σίμων. Josephus mentions a Cyprian Jew of this name, whom Felix sent to persuade Drusilla to leave her husband.

— προϋπῆρχεν, *was previously.*

— μαγεύων, *practising magical arts.*

— ἐξιστάνων, *astonishing.* ἐξιστάνω is a late form of ἐξίστημι.

10. ἀπὸ μικροῦ ἕως μεγάλου, *from small to great.* An expression which implies *all the people* of the city.

11. ἐξεστακέναι αὐτούς, *they had been bewitched.* The Authorised Version is in error here.

13. ἦν προσκαρτερῶν, *was strict in his attendance.*

— ἐξίστατο, *he was amazed.*

14. δέδεκται. The indicative is used in preference to the optative in indirect narration after a secondary tense when the writer wishes to express himself vividly.

— πρὸς αὐτούς, *to the inhabitants* of the city or the district.

16. βεβαπτισμένοι ὑπῆρχον = βεβαπτισμένοι ἦσαν.

— εἰς τὸ ὄνομα, *into the name.* The force of the preposition must be observed. Baptism is the commencement of our *union* with Christ. We are baptized *in* the Name of the Trinity, and then we become one *with* Christ.

17. ἐπετίθουν τὰς χεῖρας. This is the first mention of the rite of Confirmation, which rests mainly upon this passage and Acts xix. 6.

— Πνεῦμα ἅγιον. They probably received the miraculous gifts of the Holy Spirit, for Simon *saw* the effects.

18. προσήνεγκεν αὐτοῖς χρήματα. The term *Simony* is derived from this attempt made by Simon to purchase spiritual power.

20. εἴη. The optative is used to express a wish, *may thy silver be destined for destruction with thee.*

— κτᾶσθαι, *to purchase.*

21. μερὶς οὐδὲ κλῆρος, *part nor possession.* The words are from Deut. x. 9.

22. εἰ ἄρα, *if perchance,* implying *a doubt* as to the pardon being granted.

23. χολὴν πικρίας, *gall of bitterness, i.e.* utter depravity. See Deut. xxix. 18.

— σε ὄντα εἰς, *that thou art (fallen) into.*

25. διαμαρτυράμενοι, *having solemnly testified.* 1 aor. part. διαμαρτύρομαι, fut. διαμαρτυροῦμαι, aor. διεμαρτυράμην.

— εὐηγγελίσαντο, *they preached the gospel to.* See xiv. 21 and xvi. 10.

26. μεσημβρία for μεσημερία (from μέσος and ἡμέρα) means (1) *noon* (Thuc. vi. 100), (2) as here, *the south.*

— Γάζαν. One of the cities of the Philistines.

— αὕτη, *this road.* Philip was directed to take the less frequented of two roads which led from Jerusalem to Gaza.

27. καὶ ἰδού, *and behold, there was.*

— δυνάστης. A noun, *an officer of authority.*

— Κανδάκης. Candace was the common name of the queens of the Ethiopians of Upper Egypt, the island Meroë being probably the capital of their realm.

— γάζης, *treasure.* The Persian word γάζα, denoting *the king's treasure,* was adopted both in Greek and Latin.

— προσκυνήσων, *for the purpose of worshipping.* He was probably a Proselyte of the Gate. See note on ii. 10.

29. κολλήθητι, *join thyself.* The aorist passive is frequently used in the New Testament *in a middle sense.*

30. ἆρά γε; *do you then? num igitur?* A negative answer is expected.

30. ἃ ἀναγινώσκεις, *what thou art reading.*

31. πῶς γάρ; *why how?* γάρ is used in *earnest, urgent* questions.   Here a negative may be implied, thus (οὐ γινώσκω) πῶς γάρ = (I do not understand) for how, &c.

32. περιοχή, *passage,* or *contents.*   From περιέχω, *to contain.*

— ἀμνός, *a lamb.*   The oblique cases are seldom found, ἀρνά, ἀρνός, ἀρνί being used instead.

— τοῦ κείροντος αὐτόν, (*the man*) *shearing him.*

33. ἡ κρίσις αὐτοῦ ἤρθη, *His judgment was taken away.* He was condemned after a summary and unfair trial. The meaning of the original, Isa. liii. 8, is "He was taken away by an oppressive judgment".

— τὴν δὲ γενεάν κ.τ.λ., *and who shall declare His generation?*   The words admit two interpretations:

(1) Who shall describe the wickedness of the generation which put Him to death?

(2) Who shall describe the generation of Him who is without beginning and without end?

35. ἀνοίξας τὸ στόμα.   The expression calls attention to the gravity of the speech.   See x. 34.

36. κατὰ τὴν ὁδόν, *along the road;* lit. *down the line* of the road.

37. This verse is not found in the best MSS.; it was probably inserted to suit the Baptismal formularies of the early Church.

38. στῆναι τὸ ἅρμα, *that the chariot should stop.*

40. εὑρέθη εἰς, *was found (carried) to.*

— Ἄζωτον.   Once. called *Ashdod,* and now *Esdud,* a

town of the Philistines, in the same latitude with Jerusalem, and about thirty miles north of Gaza.

40. Καισαρίαν, *Cæsarea*, at this time the chief city in Palestine, built by Herod the Great, and named in honour of Augustus, about sixty miles from Jerusalem, on the coast. It was the residence of the Roman Procurator.

CHAPTER IX.

1. ἔτι, *still*, referring back to viii. 3.

— ἐμπνέων. Here *breathing of;* generally *breathing upon*, followed by an *accusative* of that which is breathed. Some explain the genitive as indicating that *from* which the breath was drawn.

— τῷ ἀρχιερεῖ. Taking the conversion of St. Paul to have happened in A.D. 37, the High-priest was Theophilus.

2. Damascus is first mentioned in Gen. xv. 2, where "Eliezer of Damascus," the steward of Abraham, is named. It lies in Syria, to the north-east of Palestine, in the centre of a very fertile plain about thirty miles in diameter, on the edge of the desert. At the time of the Gospel history it formed part of the kingdom of Aretas, an Arabian prince, who held his kingdom under the Romans.

— τῆς ὁδοῦ, *the Way* that leads to Salvation, an expression used several times in the Acts for Christianity, the true way to life. See xix. 9; xxii. 4.

3. περιήστραψεν, *flashed round :* for ἀστράπτω means

to flash like lightning. This took place at mid-day, and the light was brighter than sunlight (Acts xxvi. 13).

4. Σαούλ. The Hebrew form of Σαῦλε.

5. πρὸς κέντρα λακτίζειν. See xxvi. 14. These words and those which follow to ὁ κύριος πρὸς αὐτόν, are inserted in the Textus Receptus without any authority.

6. θαμβῶν, *awe-struck.*

— ὁ Κύριος πρὸς αὐτόν. Supply εἶπε.

7. εἰστήκεισαν, *were standing*, or perhaps *stopped*, for they fell afterwards to the ground, xxvi. 14.

— ἐννεοί (also written ἐνεοί), *dumb* with surprise.

— ἀκούοντες κ. τ. λ. St. Paul says (xxii. 9) that his companions *did see* the light, but that they *heard not* the voice of him that spake. This statement is quite consistent with the account here given, for probably

(1) They saw a light, but no distinct *person* (μηδένα).

(2) They heard a voice, but no distinct *words*.

8. οὐδένα, *no person.* Observe the *masculine.*

9. μὴ βλέπων, *without the power of sight.* μή is here used irregularly instead of οὐ.

11. Ταρσέα, *a native of Tarsus*, the chief city of Cilicia; a *free city*, i.e. governed by its own laws and magistrates. The river Cydnus flowed by it.

12. προσεύχεται, *he prayeth*, and is therefore no longer the enemy of Christ.

14. ὧδε, *in this place*, Damascus.

15. σκεῦος ἐκλογῆς, *a vessel of election*, i.c. a chosen vessel; the genitive of *quality.* St. Paul uses σκεῦος to express the relation in which man stands to God, as an instrument in the hands of its maker.

The word occurs with different meanings in x. 11 and xxvii. 17.

15. τοῦ βαστάσαι, *to carry*. Genitive of *purpose*.

— βασιλέων. Herod Agrippa II., and perhaps Nero.

18. εὐθέως, *immediately*. This word marks the *miraculous* nature of the cure.

— ὡσεὶ λεπίδες, *as it were scales*, i.e. something, not defined, which as a kind of film obscured his sight.

19. ἐνίσχυσεν, *he recovered his strength*. *Bodily* and (aorist) *speedily*. Compare this with verse 22.

21. ὁ πορθήσας, *who made havoc among*. The word πορθέω is properly used for *ravaging towns* or *districts*. Compare Gal. i. 13.

— ἐληλύθει ἵνα ἀγάγῃ. The optative is never used in the New Testament in final sentences.

22. ἐνεδυναμοῦτο, *was inwardly strengthened, mentally* and (imperfect) *gradually*.

— συνέχυνε, *confuted*. Imperfect συγχύνω, a late form of συγχέω, *to mix together*, and so *to confound*.

— συμβιβάζων, *proving* by a systematic argument. The word means

(1) I put together, as materials in building.

(2) I construct an argument.

Comp. xvi. 10, where the word means *drawing an inference*.

— ὁ Χριστός, *the Messiah*.

23. ἐπληροῦντο, *were approaching their completion*.

— ἡμέραι ἱκαναί. Probably referring to the time spent by St. Paul at Damascus, in Arabia, and at Damascus in his second visit (Gal. i. 18). We know from that passage that three years elapsed between St. Paul's conversion and his visit to Jerusalem. That *many days* was an expression that might include as long a period as *three years* is probable from 1 Kings ii. 38, 39.

25. καθῆκαν, *let down.* 1 aor. καθίημι.

— διὰ τοῦ τείχους, *through the wall,* i.e. through an opening in the wall, probably the window of a house attached to the city wall. See 2 Cor. xi. 33.

25. χαλάσαντες, *having lowered him.* See xxvii. 17.

26. ἐστί. The present, where we might expect the imperfect : a pure Greek construction. For the mood and tense, see note on viii. 14.

27. Barnabas and Paul were perhaps acquainted in early life, for Cyprus, the native country of Barnabas, was within sight of Cilicia.

— διηγήσατο, *explained.*

— ἐπαρρησιάσατο, *he spoke with boldness.*

30. ἐπιγνόντες, *having full knowledge (of the design).*

— κατήγαγον. Redupl. 2 aor. κατάγω, the word used for *approaching* the coast-line, ἀνάγω being used for *departing from* the coast-line. See the note on xviii. 21.

31. εἶχεν εἰρήνην. The attention of the Jews being diverted from the Christians by the attempt of Caligula to set up his statue in the Temple.

— οἰκοδομουμένη, *being built up.* A word used in the New Testament to express the growth of the Christian brotherhood in strength and grace.

— τῇ παρακλήσει, *through the exhortation.* Instrumental dat. after ἐπληθύνοντο.

32. διὰ πάντων. Supply τόπων, *through all parts*.

— Λύδδαν. Lydda, a large village near Joppa.

33. Αἰνέαν. Æneas, a Greek name (Thuc. iv. 119), not to be confounded with the Trojan Αἰνείας, Æneas.

34. στρῶσον σεαυτῷ, *make thy bed for thyself;* as an *immediate* (aorist) and *complete* proof of the cure.

35. Σαρωνᾶν. Saron or Sharon was a very fertile plain between Joppa and Cæsarea.

— οἵτινες, *so they*. More forcible than οἵ, *who*. Lat. *quippe qui*. οἵ would simply declare the fact : οἵτινες places the fact in dependence on the context. See Bp. Lightfoot on Gal. iv. 24.

36. Ἰόππῃ. Now *Jaffa*, an ancient city on the coast.

— μαθήτρια. (Att. μαθητρίς) *a female disciple*.

— Ταβειθά. An Aramaic word meaning *gazelle*, for which the Greek is δορκάς.

38. μὴ ὀκνῆσαι, *not to loiter, not to be slow*.

39. παρέστησαν, *stood by*. 2 aor. παρίστημι.

— ἐπιδεικνύμεναι, *exhibiting* (Thuc. vi. 46).

— χιτῶνας, *vests*, inner, close-fitting garments.

— ἱμάτια, *robes*, outer, loose-fitting garments.

41. παρέστησεν, *presented*. 1 aor. παρίστημι.

CHAPTER X.

1. ἑκατοντάρχης, *a centurion*, commanding the sixth part of a cohort. Favourable mention is made of the centurions throughout the whole of the New Testament, as Acts xxiii. 17, xxvii. 3 ; and Professor Blunt suggests

that this may be accounted for by the consideration that the more intelligent and orderly soldiers were probably promoted to this command.

1. σπείρης, *cohort*, made up of soldiers from *Italy*. Most of the Roman cohorts in Syria were made up of natives of the province.

2. φοβούμενος τὸν Θεόν. Some are of opinion that Cornelius was a Proselyte of the Gate, others that he was still a heathen, though *a God-fearing man.*

3. ὁράματι, *a vision*, while he was wide awake.

— ὡσεὶ ὥραν ἐννάτην, *during about the ninth hour.*

4. εἰς μνημόσυνον, *for a memorial, i.e.* so as to be observed by God.

5. ματάπεμψαι, *fetch.*

7. τῶν προσκαρτερούντων, *of those in constant attendance.*

9. ἐπὶ τὸ δῶμα, *on to the house-top*, where the Jews went for meditation and prayer.

10. πρόσπεινος, *hungry.* From πεινάω, *I am hungry.*

— γεύσασθαι, *to taste (food).*

— ἔκστασις, *a trance*, the word implying *a removal* or *rapture* of the person into a supernatural state, and so being used for the highest kind of spiritual revelation.

— σκεῦός τι, *a kind of vessel.*

11. τέσσαρσιν ἀρχαῖς, *by four corners.* Some explain ἀρχή here as meaning *the end of a rope*, comparing Eur. Hipp. 758. As a surgical word it was used for the *end of a bandage.*

— καθιέμενον, *being lowered.*

12. ἑρπετά, *creeping things; reptiles.* From ἕρπω; in Latin *serpo, I creep.*

14. οὐδέποτε ἔφαγον πᾶν, *I always abstained from eating everything.* The negative should be connected with the verb, for so the negation is made stronger.

15. ἐκαθάρισε, *made clean* or *declared to be clean,* the aorist denoting a single, definite act.

— κοίνου, *make common* or *speak of as common.* Imperat. act. κοινόω.

17. ὑπό, *by,* and not ἀπό, *from,* is the true reading.

19. διενθυμουμένου, *considering, debating within himself.*

20. ἀλλά. Elliptical (*let them seek no longer*) *but.*

22. μαρτυρούμενος, *well spoken of.* Passive.

— ἐχρηματίσθη, *was warned.* χρηματίζω means

(1) I transact business;

(2) I acquire a name, xi. 26.

— χρηματίζομαι generally means *I receive a divine warning* (Matt. ii. 12).

— ῥήματα, *words.* ῥῆμα, *detached utterance;* λόγος, *complete message,* as in verse 37.

23. καί τινες, *six* in number, as we learn from xi. 12.

24. ἦν προσδοκῶν, *was expecting.*

— ἀναγκαίους φίλους, *intimate friends;* Lat. *necessarii.*

25. ὡς ἐγένετο τοῦ εἰσελθεῖν τὸν Πέτρον, *when it came to pass that Peter entered.* The clause τοῦ εἰσελθεῖν τὸν Πέτρον is loosely used as the subject of ἐγένετο.

— προσεκύνησεν, *worshipped* (*him*); regarding him as a delegate from God.

27. συνομιλῶν, *conversing.*

28. κολλᾶσθαι, κ. τ. λ., *to join himself* or *associate with one of another nation*.

— καί, *and yet*.

29. ἀναντιρρήτως, *without making any objection*.

— μεταπεμφθείς, *when sent for*.

— πυνθάνομαι, κ. τ. λ., *I beg to know then for what reason*.

30. ἀπὸ τετάρτης ἡμέρας, *four days ago.* See xv. 7.

— ἤμην. 1 sing. imperfect *middle* of εἰμί, not Attic.

32. παραγενόμενος, *having arrived* or *on his arrival*.

33. ἐξ αὐτῆς (τῆς ὥρας), *at once*.

— ἐξαυτῆς, an adverb, for ἐξ αὐτῆς τῆς ὥρας, *at the very point of time, at once*.

— σὺ καλῶς ἐποίησας παραγενόμενος, *you acted kindly in coming*.

The aorist participle is sometimes put with a verb to denote that in which the action of the verb consists. See Plato Phaed. 60 C. εὖ ἐποίησας ἀναμνήσας με.

35. δεκτός, *acceptable* rather than *accepted*.

36. τὸν λόγον seems to be governed by ὑμεῖς οἴδατε in verse 37. But if ὅν be omitted (as in some of the best MSS.) τὸν λόγον is governed by ἀπέστειλεν.

In translating 36 to 38 (if ὅν be retained) it seems best to supply ὑμεῖς οἴδατε at the commencement of vv. 36 and 38.

37. ῥῆμα, *story* or *account*.

— γενόμενον, *which was spoken of* or *which was published*.

38. ἔχρισεν, *anointed.* 1 aor. χρίω.

— καταδυναστευομένους, *overpowered*.

39. ἀνεῖλον κρεμάσαντες, *they slew by hanging.* Compare chap. v. 30. The participle is used to express the *means* by which an action is performed.

41. προκεχειροτονημένοις, *appointed beforehand.*

42. διαμαρτύρασθαι, *to testify solemnly.*

— ὡρισμένος, *appointed.*

43. τούτῳ, *to this Person.*

44. τὰ ῥήματα ταῦτα, *these words.*

45. ἐξέστησαν, *were astonished.*

— οἱ ἐκ περιτομῆς πιστοί, *the faithful of the circumcision, i.e.* the Jewish converts to Christianity.

— ἐκκέχυται. In a causal sentence, when the cause is assigned by some other person than the speaker, the *tense* originally used by the person who assigned the cause is used, but generally in the optative *mood;* see Thuc. ii. 21. The indicative is used for vividness; see viii. 14.

46. γλώσσαις. Probably the same as ἑτέραις γλώσσαις in ii. 4.

47. μήτι δύναταί τις; *can any one?* μήτι is used in questions where an affirmative answer would be absurd. Compare Matt. vii. 16.

CHAPTER XI.

1. ἐδέξαντο. Aorist, where we should expect the pluperfect, a usage not uncommon in relative clauses (as in Acts i. 2), and in clauses introduced by ὅτι.

2. διεκρίνοντο, *raised a discussion.*

4

2. οἱ ἐκ περιτομῆς, *they of the circumcision;* ἐκ denoting *the class* to which they belonged, the Jewish converts to Christianity.

4. ἐξετίθετο, *proceeded to make an explanation.*

— καθεξῆς, *in regular order.* See iii. 24.

8. πᾶν. Not found in the best MSS. If it be retained, the negative and the verb must be closely connected; *everything common or unclean never at any time entered.*

10. ἀνεσπάσθη ἅπαντα. Singular verb with neuter plural nominative.

14. ἐν οἷς may be rendered *by which,* but observe that the *ground* rather than the *means* of salvation is implied.

15. ἄρξασθαι is not redundant, the meaning being *scarcely had I commenced my speech, when the Holy Spirit fell on them.*

16. ὡς ἔλεγεν is not redundant, but is added for *circum-stantiality.* Thucydides often uses the imperfect ἔλεγον for the aorist.

17. ἐγὼ δὲ τίς ἤμην δυνατός; Here two interrogatory clauses are blended, the meaning being, *but I, who was I? Had I power to withstand God?*

18. ἄραγε, *so then, in that case* (γε) *we may conclude that* (ἄρα).

— εἰς ζωήν, *unto life,* εἰς denoting the *end* or *aim* of an action.

19. διασπαρέντες, *scattered about.* The narrative in viii. 3 is now resumed.

— ἀπὸ τῆς θλίψεως, *owing to the persecution.* The persecution being the occasion of their departure.

— ἐπὶ Στεφάνῳ seems to mean *over, on account of,* or *in reference to Stephen.*

20. Ἑλληνιστάς. For which many editors put "Ἕλλη-νας. The MSS. afford no certain evidence. The question is interesting on this account, that if "Ἕλληνας be the true reading (as it probably is), Cornelius was not *the first Gentile convert*, since the events here recorded took place apparently before his conversion.

23. προσμένειν, *to wait still longer for*, or *to cleave to*.

25. Antioch stood on the river Orontes, about seventeen miles from Seleucia, its port. Under the Romans it was the residence of the Proconsul of Syria. In the fifth century it was regarded as the third city in the world, ranking next after Rome and Alexandria.

26. ἐγένετο αὐτοὺς συναχθῆναι, *it came to pass that they were associated*. The use of the accusative with the infinitive in the New Testament is comparatively rare, most of the instances being in St. Luke's writings, and especially after ἐγένετο. συνέβη is used in this way with the acc. and infin. in Attic, and such is the construction in Acts xxi. 35. Compare Thuc. viii. 25.

— χρηματίσαι, *gained the name*. The usual meaning of χρηματίζω is *I transact business*, but in late Greek it means *I gain a name* from the business I follow.

Compare Rom. vii. 3, and also, for the *passive*, Acts x. 22.

— Χριστιανούς. The word only occurs in two other passages in the New Testament.

(1) Acts xxvi. 28. "With little trouble thou wouldest fain make me a Christian."

(2) 1 Pet. iv. 16. "If any man suffer as a Christian, let him not be ashamed."

The Christians called themselves οἱ μαθηταί, οἱ πιστόι, οἱ ἀδελφόι, οἱ ἅγιοι.

The Jews called them Galilæans, Nazarenes.

The Romans called them *Christiani*, "followers of Christus".

27. προφῆται. This word does not necessarily refer to men who had the power of foretelling future events; it is used in several passages for persons gifted with a miraculous power of *interpreting* Scripture. See also xiii. 1.

28. λιμὸν μέγαν. The true reading is μεγάλην, since λιμός was of the *feminine* gender in Doric and in the later Greek.

— ὅλην τὴν οἰκουμένην (γῆν), *the whole inhabited (world)*. There were many *local* famines in the days of Claudius, and one especially affected Judæa in the 4th year of his reign.

29. ηὐπορεῖτο, *was in good circumstances*.

30. πρεσβυτέρους. Presbyters are here mentioned for the first time. In the New Testament the words ἐπίσκοπος and πρεσβύτερος are applied indifferently to the same persons, as may be seen from Acts xx. 17 and 28. *After the Apostolic times* one of the πρεσβύτεροι was chosen to preside over each Church, and to him was given the title ἐπίσκοπος.

CHAPTER XII.

1. Ἡρώδης. Herod Agrippa I., son of Aristobulus, and grandson of Herod the Great. Caligula gave him the tetrarchy of Philip, and the title of King. Claudius

gave him Samaria and Judæa, so that at this time he reigned over all the kingdom of Herod the Great.

Josephus gives him a high character, saying that he was liberal, gentle, and compassionate, and that he was strongly attached to the Jewish Law, which probably accounts for his spite against the Christians.

— κακῶσαι, *to maltreat.*

— ἀπό, denoting *the class* to which the sufferers belonged, is in the phrase οἱ ἀπὸ Πλάτωνος, *the school of Plato.*

2. Ἰάκωβον. James, the son of Zebedee, was one of the three favoured Apostles who were present at the raising of the daughter of Jairus, at the Transfiguration, and at the Agony in the Garden of Gethsemane. He is the only Apostle of whose death we have any *certain* record.

3. προσέθετο, *he proceeded further.*

— τῶν ἀζύμων, *of unleavened (bread).* The word to be supplied is λαγάνων. The broad flat cakes into which the Paschal Bread was made were called λάγανα. It is necessary to supply *a neuter* substantive, because τὰ ἄζυμα is the New Testament expression for the Feast of Unleavened Bread, which lasted from the 14th to the 21st of the month Nisan.

4. πιάσας, *having taken.* From πιάζω, iii. 7.

— παραδούς. After this word take αὐτόν, *having delivered him to four quaternions of soldiers to guard.* This use of the infinitive, to express a *purpose*, instead of ὥστε with the infinitive, is common in the New Testament. See v. 31; xx. 28. For instances of παραδίδωμι followed by the infinitive, see Eur. Or. 64, and Thuc. viii. 28.

4. τέσσαρσι τετραδίοις.   One quaternion for each watch of the night.   Of the *four* men, forming the quaternion, *two* were probably stationed outside the prison, and *two* were chained to the prisoner (see verse 6).

— τὸ πάσχα.   From a Hebrew word signifying *a passing over*.   When the Lord slew the firstborn of the Egyptians, the Israelites were directed to sprinkle the doorposts of their houses with the blood of a lamb : and God said, " When I see the blood, I will *pass over* you " (Exod. xii. 13).   The Jews ate the Paschal Feast on the 14th of Nisan, but here the term includes the days of Unleavened Bread.

5. ἐκτενής, *fervent*.   The word means literally *stretched out, strained*.

6. ἁλύσεσι δυσί, *with two chains*, attached by a chain to each of the two soldiers.   Compare xxi. 33 and xxviii. 16, 20, in the latter passage the singular ἅλυσιν being used, because St. Paul had only *one* soldier to guard him.

7. ἐπέστη, *came suddenly*.   See iv. 1.

— οἰκήματι, *chamber* or *cell*.

8. ζῶσαι, *gird thyself*.   The tunic (χιτών) was a closely-fitting garment, resembling in form and use our shirt, kept close to the body *by a girdle*.

— ὑπόδησαι, *bind on* (*thy feet*).   1 aor. imperat. mid. ὑποδέω, *I bind under*.

— σανδάλια.   Diminutive of σάνδαλον, a wooden sole, firmly bound on by straps round the instep and ankle.

— περιβαλοῦ, *cast round thyself*, the outer *robe* (ἱμάτιον), a quadrangular piece of woollen cloth, resembling in shape a Scotch plaid.

9. ἀληθές, a reality.

— τὸ γινόμενον, that which was being done.

11. γενόμενος ἐν ἑαυτῷ, having come to his senses, having recovered from his bewilderment.

— ἐξαπέστειλε, sent, aorist.

— ἐξείλατο, delivered, aorist.

12. συνιδών, being aware of it, being fully conscious that he was really free.

— Μάρκου. Probably St. Mark the Evangelist. He is mentioned again in xii. 25 and xv. 37. St. Peter speaks of him as " Marcus, my son " (1 Pet. v. 13), whence some have concluded that St. Peter converted Mark. He was the cousin (ἀνεψιός) of Barnabas (Col. iv. 10).

13. τοῦ πυλῶνος may mean the gate, or more probably the porch, the passage from the street into the first court of the house.

— ὑπακοῦσαι, to answer. A word used in classical Greek for the porter's answering a knock at the door.

14. ἑστάναι, was standing. Perfect. infin. ἵστημι.

15. διϊσχυρίζετο, persisted in affirming.

— ἄγγελος αὐτοῦ. It was a received opinion among the devout Jews that every person had his Guardian Angel, who sometimes appeared in the person's shape. Compare Matt. xviii. 10.

16. ἐπέμενε κρούων, knocked persistingly.

— ἐξέστησαν, were astonished.

17. κατασείσας, having motioned. Especially used for making a motion with the hand to produce silence. See note on xix. 33.

— Ἰακώβῳ. This James was one of the persons called brothers of our Lord (Matt. xiii. 55 ; Gal. i. 19).

He was probably the first Bishop of Jerusalem, where he was killed in a popular tumult, being hurled down from the Temple.

18. ἄρα, which really means *then, under these circumstances*, is here perhaps used in the sense of *possibly*, giving emphasis to τί.

— τί ὁ Πέτρος ἐγένετο ; *what had become of Peter? what was the position (in which) Peter was?*

19. ἀνακρίνας, *having examined*.

— ἀπαχθῆναι, *to be led away (to execution)*.

— διέτριβεν (χρόνον), *he was passing (the time there)*.

20. θυμομαχῶν, *highly displeased*, though not at actual war.

— τὸν ἐπὶ τοῦ κοιτῶνος, *who had charge of the bedchamber*.

— τρέφεσθαι, *was supported* to *some* extent (which is implied by ἀπό being used instead of ὑπό) by the supplies of corn sent by Herod's subjects. So also we find that Solomon made presents of wheat to Hiram, king of Tyre, in return for cedars.

21. τοῦ βήματος, *the tribunal*, a raised seat from which an assembly might be addressed. The scene of these proceedings was the Theatre. The date, very important to the chronology of this book, was A.D. 44.

25. Βαρνάβας . . . Σαῦλος. At this time, Barnabas, as the senior disciple, and perhaps as higher in office in the Church (see xiii. 1), takes *precedence* of Paul. After the infliction of blindness on Elymas (xiii. 11) Paul is *usually* put first.

— τὴν διακονίαν, *their ministration*, to carry up alms from Antioch for the assistance of the brethren in Judæa during the famine. See xi. 29, 30.

CHAPTER XIII.

1. προφῆται καὶ διδάσκαλοι. The same words for Church officers are used by St. Paul in 1 Cor. xii. 28 : "First Apostles, secondarily Prophets, thirdly Teachers". The προφῆται then appear to have been higher in rank than the διδάσκαλοι. Now of the five persons mentioned in this verse, it appears from the arrangement of the conjunctions τε . . . τε, that *three* (Barnabas, Symeon, and Lucius) were προφῆται, and *two* (Manaen and Saul) διδάσκαλοι.

— Lucius may be the person mentioned by St. Paul in Rom. xvi. 21.

— Herod the Tetrarch, Herod Antipas, at this time living in exile at Lyons.

— σύντροφος, *foster-brother.*

2. λειτουργούντων, *performing official duties.* In classical Greek the word λειτουργία denotes any *public service*, whether of a secular or religious nature.

— ἀφορίσατε δή, *set apart at once.*

— εἰς τὸ ἔργον (εἰς) ὅ, *to the work to which.*

— προσκέκλημαι, middle, *have called them for Myself.*

3. νηστεύσαντες καὶ προσευξάμενοι. Fasting and prayer have always preceded the seasons of Ordination, but the *Ember* Fasts were not appointed till the fourth century.

— ἐπιθέντες. The *second* instance of Ordination. See vi. 6.

4. Seleucia, a city near the mouth of the Orontes, seventeen miles, by land, from Antioch.

5. Salamis, a town on the *eastern* side of Cyprus, founded by a colony from the more famous Salamis in the Saronic Gulf.

6. διελθόντες, *having gone right through*, from east to west, one hundred miles.

— Paphos was on the western shore of the island. It was a few miles distant from the old town of the same name, famous for the temple and worship of Venus.

— μάγον. The word μάγος was applied to the class of priests and wise men in Persia, who interpreted dreams. Hence it was used for pretenders to the power of foretelling and influencing future events. Such persons were much in repute among the Roman nobility in St. Paul's age.

7. ἀνθυπάτῳ, *proconsul*. The Roman Provinces were divided by Augustus into two classes; some he retained under his own *military* government, others he resigned to the *civil* government of the Senate. The Emperor's provinces were governed by Legati, or, as they were sometimes called, *Propraetors* (ἀντιστράτηγοι); the Senatorial Provinces were governed by *Proconsuls* (ἀνθύπατοι). Cyprus was at first retained by Augustus, but afterwards he assigned it to the *Senate*, and therefore the title given by St. Luke to the governor is strictly correct.

8. Ἐλύμας ὁ μάγος. Elymas is an Arabic name, meaning *wise man*, and is therefore equivalent to ὁ μάγος. Render the verse thus: "But Elymas, the wise man, for so his name is interpreted, withstood them ".

— διαστρέφειν, *to warp, or distort, to wrest out of the straight (right) line or proper direction, to pervert or deprave the judgment.* Cope on Arist. Rhet. A. 1, 5.

9. ὁ καὶ Παῦλος. ὁ is not put for ὅς, but καλούμενος is to be supplied.

The change of names from *Saul* to *Paul* may have been made—

(1) To indicate the change wrought in the Apostle; he who was once a Jew was now a Christian; he who was once a Persecutor was now a Preacher.

(2) Because Saul was a purely *Jewish* name, and the name Paul, while retaining somewhat of his original name, was more suited to the ears of the Gentiles.

10. ῥᾳδιουργίας, *recklessness*. The word, from ῥᾴδιος, and ἔργον, means (1) facility of action, (2) levity or recklessness of conduct. Compare xviii. 14.

11. ἀχλὺς καὶ σκότος. First a *dimness*, and then total *darkness;* or simply mist and darkness as *cause* and *effect*.

— περιάγω, *I lead round*, has also in classical Greek an intransitive meaning, *I go round*, as here: it is followed by an accusative in Mark vi. 6.

12. ἐκπλησσόμενος, *being struck with amazement*.

13. ἀναχθέντες, *having put out to sea*. See note on ix. 30.

— οἱ περὶ τὸν Παῦλον, *Paul and his companions*. The phrase (only here in N. T.) *includes* Paul, as it specifies those who *surrounded* him.

— Ἰωάνης. In the last Epistle written by St. Paul we have a proof that St. Mark was reconciled to him. "Having taken Mark, bring him with thee, for he is profitable unto me for the ministry" (2 Tim. iv. 11).

15. τὴν ἀνάγνωσιν, *the reading*. The custom of read-

ing the Law to the congregation commenced after the
Captivities. Antiochus Epiphanes compelled the Jews
to relinquish the reading of the Law, and then they read
the Prophets instead ; and *both* were read after the delivery of the nation by Judas Maccabæus.

15. ἀρχισυνάγωγοι. Elders who managed the regula-
tions of the services.

— παρακλήσεως, *exhortation* or *consolation;* here
probably the former.

16. κατασείσας, *having motioned them to silence.* See
xii. 17.

17. ἐξελέξατο, *selected.* Compare xv. 22.

— βραχίονος ὑψηλοῦ, *a lofty arm*, a Hebrew expression for great display of strength. Compare Isa. liii. 1,
" to whom is the arm of the Lord revealed? " and Ex.
vi. 6, " I will redeem you with a stretched out arm (ἐν
βραχίονι ὑψηλῷ in the LXX.).

18. ὡς τεσσαρακονταετῆ χρόνον, *during the space of
about forty years.*

— ἐτροποφόρησεν αὐτούς, *He bore with their manners;*
but another reading is ἐτροφοφόρησεν, *He nourished,*
which is probably correct.

19. κατεκληροδότησεν, *He distributed by lot;* but the
true reading is κατεκληρονόμησεν, *gave as an inheritance.*

20. A considerable difficulty in chronology is raised
by this verse. In 1 Kings vi. 1, it is said that Solomon
commenced his Temple 480 years after the Exodus.
Saul and David reigned eighty years, and the Exodus
was many years before the time of the first Judge. On
the other hand, the duration of government assigned to
the Judges makes up about 450 years, and St. Paul

probably follows here the *apparent* chronology of the
Book of Judges.   But it is not at all certain that the
history in that book is *consecutive history*, for deliverances
may have been wrought *at the same time in different parts
of the land*.

The great MSS. have a reading which solves, or perhaps evades, the difficulty; in them καὶ μετὰ ταῦτα is
put *after* πεντήκοντα.

21. κἀκεῖθεν = καὶ ἐκεῖθεν, *and after that*.

22. μεταστήσας, *having deposed*.

— ᾧ μαρτυρήσας, *by way of testimony to whom*.

24. πρὸ προσώπου τῆς εἰσόδου αὐτοῦ, *before the face of
His coming*, meaning, "before Christ entered into public
life".   The form of the expression is Hebraistic.

25. ἐπλήρου.   Imperfect, *was fulfilling*, i.e. was bringing to a conclusion.

26. ἡμῖν (not ὑμῖν) is the true reading.

— τῆς σωτηρίας ταύτης, *of this salvation*, referring to
σωτῆρα in verse 23.

— ἐξαπεστάλη, *was sent forth*.

27. τὰς . . . ἀναγινωσκομένας, *that are read*.   See
note on verse 15.

— κρίναντες (τοῦτον) ἐπλήρωσαν (τὰς φωνάς), *having
judged (Him) fulfilled (them)*.

28. Πιλάτον.   Pontius Pilate was Procurator of
Judæa for ten years.   He resided at Cæsarea, coming
up at certain seasons to Jerusalem.   At the expiration
of his government he was accused of extortion, and
went into exile.

— ἀναιρεθῆναι αὐτόν, *that He might be put to death*.

29. ἐτέλεσαν, *they had accomplished.* The aorist is put for the pluperfect in secondary clauses in which *time* is specified. So in Latin *postquam venit = after he had come.*

32. εὐαγγελιζόμεθα. Here *only* followed by two accusatives, ὑμᾶς . . . ἐπαγγελίαν.

— τοῖς τέκνοις ἡμῶν, *to our children,* but probably ἡμῖν should be read for ἡμῶν.

33. δευτέρῳ. The original reading seems to have been πρώτῳ. The words are in our *Second* Psalm, but it was originally one with the *First,* or rather the First Psalm was an introduction to the Psalter.

34. ὅτι δέ, *and (to shew) that.*

— τὰ ὅσια τὰ πιστά, *the holy, the sure (mercies).* The kindnesses bestowed on David are called ὅσια as proceeding from God, and πιστά as promised by God.

36. ἰδίᾳ γενεᾷ ὑπηρετήσας, *having ministered to his own generation.*

39. ἀπὸ πάντων (ἀφ᾽) ὧν, *from all things from which.* Compare verse 2.

— ἐν τῷ νόμῳ, *in (i.e. under) the Law,* not *causal* but *local.*

— ἐν τούτῳ, *in (i.e. by union with) Christ.*

— δικαιοῦται, *is justified,* i.e. absolved from guilt.

40. προφήταις. The plural is used because the speaker does not choose to specify the particular prophet, in this case Habakkuk i. 5.

42. ἐξιόντων, κ.τ.λ. With the reading of the received text, which is here very corrupt, we must render, *when the Jews were departing from the synagogue.*

42. τὸ μεταξὺ σάββατον, *the next Sabbath.* This use of μεταξύ, which commonly means *intervening*, is found only in later Greek.

43. ἐπιμένειν (or, as some read, προσμένειν), *to cleave to;* when used thus it takes the dative.

44. ἐρχομένῳ, the more probable reading is ἐχομένῳ. Either would mean *the next.*

45. ἀντιλέγοντες, *contradicting.* Repetition of the verbal notion for emphasis.

47. ἐντέταλται. Perf. pass. ἐντέλλω, with a middle signification.

— τοῦ εἶναι. Genitive of *purpose.* Thuc. i. 4.

48. ἦσαν τεταγμένοι, *had been appointed.* Taking it as *passive* it may yet refer merely to an Election to *Grace,* and not (as Calvin maintains) to an Election to *Glory.* Some would take it in a *middle* sense, *had set themselves towards,* comparing the use of διατεταγμένος in xx. 13.

50. εὐσχήμονας, *of honourable rank,* a meaning of the word in *late* Greek.

51. ἐκτιναξάμενοι. As commanded by our Lord (Mark vi. 11). The Jews carefully removed the dust from their shoes when they came from another country over the frontier of the Holy Land.

— Ἰκόνιον. Iconium, at this time capital of *Lycaonia,* was a populous city at the foot of Mount Taurus.

CHAPTER XIV.

1. κατὰ τὸ αὐτό, *at the same time, i.e. together.*

— Ἑλλήνων. Probably Proselytes of the Gate.

2. ἐκάκωσαν, *rendered malevolent, provoked to anger*.

3. ἐπὶ τῷ Κυρίῳ, *in reliance on the Lord*.

— τῷ μαρτυροῦντι τῷ λόγῳ, *who gave testimony to the word*.

— διδόντι, *by giving*. καί should be omitted, the participle expressing the *means* by which a result is obtained.

5. ὁρμή, *an impulse*. Referring not to an actual *attack*, but to the *first stir* of excitement that would have led to an assault.

6. συνιδόντες, *being aware of it*.

— κατέφυγον, *they escaped*.

9. τοῦ σωθῆναι. The genitive is used as depending on the noun πίστιν.

10. ἥλλετο, *he began to leap*. Imperfect, ἅλλομαι, but the true reading is ἥλατο, aorist, *he sprang up*.

— περιεπάτει, *he began to walk*.

11. Λυκαονιστί, *in the language of Lycaonia*, an Assyrian dialect.

Adverbs, which express *after the manner of*, end in ι ; hence such adverbs are used to express the following of *customs* or *language ;* thus Ἑλληνιστί, *after Greek fashion*, is employed (xxi. 37) for *speaking in the Greek language*.

12. Ἑρμῆν. Hermes, messenger of the Gods, and (in later mythology) himself the God of *Eloquence :* whence they identified St. Paul with him, because that Apostle took the lead in the speaking.

— αὐτός, emphatic, *he, as leader*.

13. τοῦ Διός, *of Zeus ;* the name of the *God* put for the *temple*. Compare *Lays of Ancient Rome :*

> " From Castor in the Forum
> To Mars without the wall ".

13. στέμματα, *garlands* to deck the priests and the victims.

— πυλῶνας, *gates* of the house in which the Apostles lodged.

14. διαρρήξαντες, *having rent.* The Jews *rent* their garments on hearing expressions which they regarded as *blasphemy.*

15. ὁμοιοπαθεῖς, *of like affections,* such as joy and sorrow.

— εὐαγγελιζόμενοι, *preaching the glad tidings.*

— ὑμᾶς, *to you;* ἐπιστρέφειν, *that you should turn.* This use of the simple infinitive to express a *result* is often found in Homer; but it is not an Attic construction. But see note on xv. 20.

16. παρῳχημέναις, *past.* Perf. part. pass. παροίχομαι, *I have passed by.*

17. καίτοι, *and yet.*

— ἀμάρτυρον, *without witness,* as in Thuc. ii. 41.

— οὐκ ἀφῆκεν, *he did not leave.*

— ὑετούς, *rain.* Lycaonia was much afflicted by *drought.*

18. κατέπαυσαν . . . τοῦ μὴ θύειν, *restrained . . . from sacrificing.* With verbs expressing *denial* or *preventing,* the infinitive is used with μή, contrary to our idiom, to strengthen the negation.

19. ἔσυρον, *they dragged* with violence. Compare viii. 3.

— τεθνάναι. Contracted form of τεθνηκέναι.

21. μαθητεύσαντες ἱκανούς, *having made disciples of*

5

many. In classical Greek μαθητεύω means, *I am a pupil;* in later Greek it was used as a *transitive* verb.

22. ἐπιστηρίζοντες, *confirming.*

— ἐμμένειν, *to abide in.*

— καὶ ὅτι . . . δεῖ ἡμᾶς, *and (saying) we must.* Observe the change from the indirect to the direct narration, and see note on i. 4.

23. χειροτονήσαντες, *having appointed.* The word properly means *to elect by a show of hands.*

— κατ' ἐκκλησίαν, *in each Church.* Distributive force of κατά. Compare Tit. i. 5.

— πεπιστεύκεισαν. The *omission of the augment* in the *pluperfect* is not uncommon in Attic.

25. Ἀτταλίαν. A town in Pamphylia, on the coast.

— κἀκεῖθεν, *and from that place.*

— ὅθεν ἦσαν παραδεδομένοι, *from which place they had been intrusted.*

— ὃ ἐπλήρωσαν, *which they had fulfilled.* Aorist for pluperfect. See xiii. 29.

27. θύραν πίστεως, *a door of faith,* i.e. an opening for preaching of the Gospel. A similar expression is used by St. Paul in 1 Cor. xvi. 9.

CHAPTER XV.

1. The events recorded in this chapter happened in A.D. 50. The middle of the Acts corresponds with the middle of the century.

— κατελθόντες, *having come down* to Antioch.

1. τῷ ἔθει, *in accordance with the custom.* Dative of *custom* or *rule.*

2. τῷ Παύλῳ, *for Paul.* Dative of *especial reference,* depending on γενομένης. See ii. 43.

— αὐτούς. Refers to the Judaizing teachers, and a new subject must be supplied with ἔταξαν, thus, (*the members of the Church*) *determined.*

3. προπεμφθέντες, *having been escorted.* Compare xxi. 5, and observe carefully the force of the preposition. Lat. *deducti.*

— ἐκδιηγούμενοι, *describing fully.* Lat. *accurate enarrantes.*

4. παρεδέχθησαν, *they were received.* Implying a reception of the deputation in its *official* character.

5. πεπιστευκότες, *who had become believers.*

— δεῖ περιτέμνειν αὐτούς, *one must circumcise them.* Observe the *active.*

6. ἰδεῖν, *to make investigation.*

7. ἀφ' ἡμερῶν ἀρχαίων, *from days long past.* ἀπό frequently designates the *commencement of a period.* The conversion of Cornelius, which took place about fifteen years before, is here referred to.

— ἐν ἡμῖν ἐξελέξατο, *made a selection among us.* His meaning is explained by what follows : *he* was chosen to be first among the Apostles to preach to the Gentiles.

8. ἐμαρτύρησεν αὐτοῖς, *bore witness in their favour;* testified to their fitness for the privilege conferred upon them. Compare xiii. 22.

10. πειράζετε. Men are said to tempt God, when, by opposing His declared will, they vainly try to alter His settled purpose.

10. ἐπιθεῖναι, *by placing*. The infinitive is loosely used to express the *result* or, as here, *the way of carrying into effect*. See note on xiv. 15.

11. κἀκεῖνοι = καὶ ἐκεῖνοι (πιστεύουσι σωθῆναι), *they also (believe that they are saved)*.

13. ἀπεκρίθη, *took up the discourse*.

14. Συμεών, the Hebrew form of Σιμών; used also in 2 Peter i. 1.

— ἐξηγήσατο, *explained* in the speech just delivered.

— καθώς, *in what manner*, with some emphasis, the *precise* way in which.

— ἐπεσκέψατο, *visited*. The meanings of this verb are thus arranged:

(1) I look closely into.

(2) I select after enquiry (Acts vi. 3).

(3) I visit a person to see how he fares (Acts xv. 36).

(4) I visit, with a view to do a kindness to a person, as here.

15. τούτῳ. Neuter, *with this*.

16. ἀναστρέψω, *I will turn myself again*, as opposed to His turning away from them. Compare vii. 42.

— τὰ κατεσκαμμένα, *the ruins*. From κατασκάπτω, *I dig down*. Some read κατεστραμμένα, with the same meaning.

17. This verse is nearly a literal quotation from the Septuagint Version of Amos ix. 12.

The original Hebrew differs widely from it, and is thus rendered in the English Version, " That they may possess the remnant of Edom, and of all the heathen, which are called by My name ".

17. ἐφ᾽ οὕς, κ.τ.λ. "*Over* whom My name has been called *over* them;" which means, "Over whom My name has been pronounced, so that they derive the name of God's people from it". Compare James ii. 7.

— ἐπ᾽ αὐτούς. A repetition for *perspicuity* or *emphasis*.

18. ἀπ᾽ αἰῶνος, *from the first beginning*.

19. κρίνω, *I am of opinion*. Lat. *censeo*.

— παρενοχλεῖν, *to trouble in the matter*. παρενοχλέω means *I give annoyance to one who is engaged in some business*.

— ἐπιστρέφουσιν, *who are turning*.

20. ἐπιστεῖλαι, *to send a command in writing*.

— τοῦ ἀπέχεσθαι, *that they should abstain*. The genitive expresses the *design* or *scope* of the letter. The genitive of the infinitive with τοῦ implies simply a connexion in the *attached* notion with respect to that which *precedes* it. Generally *design* is implied, but sometimes *result*. See Thuc. ii. 4.

— ἀλισγημάτων, *pollutions*. From ἀλισγέω, *I pollute*; a word of late Greek.

— τοῦ αἵματος. This ancient prohibition, first imposed on Noah, was renewed by the Mosaic Law: "Ye shall eat the blood of no manner of flesh" (Lev. xvii. 14).

21. γάρ. The reason for the prohibition is now given; that no offence should be given by the Gentile converts to the Jewish Christians, who were constantly being reminded of the prohibitions by hearing the Books of Moses read in the synagogues.

21. ἐκ γενεῶν ἀρχαίων, *from generations of old*, i.e. from ancient times.

— τοὺς κηρύσσοντας αὐτόν, *those who preach* (or *proclaim*) *him*; those who by reading the Law teach men to look up to Moses as their guide in such matters.

22. ἐκλεξαμένους, *that they having selected*. This must not be translated as if it were *passive*, as in the Authorised Version. The *accusative* of the participle with the infinitive follows the *dative* in the best authors, e.g. Thuc. vii. 57 ; Herod iii. 25.

— τῷ Παύλῳ καὶ Βαρνάβᾳ. In a series of nouns forming one compound statement, only the *first* has the Article. See i. 13.

When each of the connected nouns is to be regarded as independent, the Article is generally put with each. See xv. 6 and xxvi. 30.

— Silas, called by St. Paul Silvanus, was with the Apostle in his second missionary journey.

Silvanus, who is mentioned as a companion of St. Peter (1 Pet. v. 12), *may be* the same person.

23. γράψαντες. This, for γράψαντας, is a clear instance of *anakoluthon*, a term which denotes that the construction with which a sentence is begun is not carried out.

— χαίρειν, with the ellipsis of κελεύουσι, *bid you hail*, *salvere jubent*.

This infinitive usually stands alone at the beginning of letters. See xxiii. 26.

24. ἀνασκευάζοντες, *unsettling*. ἀνασκευάζω, *I unfurnish* (the opposite of κατασκευάζω, *I furnish*), is used in

classical Greek for *dismantling a city*, and generally for ravaging or destroying.

25. γενομένοις ὁμοθυμαδόν, *since we were of one mind.* The verbs εἶναι, γίγνεσθαι, and φῦναι are frequently used in this way with *adverbs.* See Herod. vi. 109.

— ἐκλεξαμένους, *that we having selected.* See verse 22.

26. παραδεδωκόσι, *have given up.* They exposed themselves freely to death, and so gave up their lives *in will* for the cause of Christ.

27. ἀπαγγέλλοντας, *announcing.* The *present* is used, as the letter, when read, would refer to the fact as *then present.*

— διὰ λόγου, *by word of mouth.*

28. τῶν ἐπάναγκες (ὄντων), *that are necessary.* Ἐπάναγκες is properly a neuter adjective, but it is frequently used as an adverb. Three great MSS. read ἐπ' ἀνάγκαις.

29. εἰδωλοθύτων, *things offered to idols*, the flesh of victims sacrificed in the Heathen Temples, which was eaten at feasts after the sacrifices, or sold in the public market. St. Paul removed this restriction to a certain extent (1 Cor. viii.).

— διατηροῦντες, *carefully guarding.*

— ἔῤῥωσθε, *fare-well.* The imperative of the perf. mid. and pass. of ῥώννυμι. The usual termination of a letter.

30. τὸ πλῆθος, *the main body* of the Christians.

31. ἀναγνόντες δέ, *and having read it.*

— παρακλήσει, *exhortation* or *consolation.* Here probably the former.

32. αὐτοί. Emphatic; no less than Paul and Barnabas.

34. ἐπιμεῖναι, to remain a longer time; diutius commorari.

Verse 34 is not found in the chief MSS.

35. διέτριβον (χρόνον), were passing (the time).

36. δή, forthwith, expressive of an energetic appeal. Compare xiii. 2.

— κατὰ πᾶσαν πόλιν, ἐν αἷς, in every one of the cities, in which. The plural follows naturally after the distributive κατά.

— πῶς ἔχουσι, (to see) how they fare. To see is implied in ἐπισκεψώμεθα.

37. ἐβουλεύσατο, purposed, formed a plan. Compare xxvii. 39.

38. ἠξίου, thought it right. Imperfect of ἀξιόω.

— ἀπὸ Παμφυλίας, from Pamphylia, i.e. as they were leaving Pamphylia.

— μή. Of the negative particles, οὐ is used when something is denied in plain terms and directly (as a matter of fact); μή, when something is denied as mere matter of thought (according to supposition and under conditions). Compare 24 with this verse.

— τοῦτον, this man. The pronoun is inserted for the sake of emphasis.

39. παροξυσμός, exasperation, sharp contention. Observe that St. Paul makes kindly mention of St. Barnabas in a letter written after this quarrel (1 Cor. ix. 6).

CHAPTER XVI.

1. κατήντησε, *he arrived.* 1 aor. καταντάω, a word of late Greek.

— ἰδού, adverb, *behold! lo!*
ἰδοῦ, imperat. mid. of the aorist εἶδον. }

— ἐκεῖ. In Lystra.

— Timotheus was with St. Paul in his second and third journeys, and during his imprisonment at Rome. We then find him at the head of the Church at Ephesus, receiving the two last letters written by St. Paul. Tradition ascribes martyrdom to him in the reign of Domitian.

— πιστῆς, *a believer.* Her name was Eunice. See 2 Tim. i. 5.

— Ἕλληνος, *a Greek.* The word does not necessarily imply that he was a heathen, for it might stand for one who was a Proselyte of the Gate. See note on ii. 10.

2. ἐμαρτυρεῖτο, *was well spoken of.* See vi. 3.

3. διὰ τοὺς Ἰουδαίους. That he might not put a stumbling-block in the way of the Jews by having one with him who, though by birth a Jew, was uncircumcised. In the case of Titus, a Greek, St. Paul refused to circumcise him (Gal. ii. 3).

4. Notice the imperfects διεπορεύοντο and παρεδίδοσαν.

— αὐτοῖς, *to the inhabitants,* i.e. to the *Gentile* converts in the cities.

— τὰ κεκριμένα, *that had been judicially appointed.*

6. τὴν Φρυγίαν. In the western part of Central Asia Minor. No precise geographical boundaries can be assigned to this district, which contributed portions, varying at different times, to several Roman provinces. Colossæ was one of its principal towns.

— τὴν Γαλατικὴν χώραν. The midland district of Asia Minor, known also as Gallo-Græcia, because it was inhabited by a mixed population of Greeks and those Gauls who invaded Asia in the third century B.C. Observe that χώραν is used because a distinct *geographical* district is meant : and compare xviii. 23.

7. οὐκ εἴασεν, *did not permit*. 1 aor. ἐάω.

8. Τρωάδα. Troas, one of the most important towns of the province of Asia. Its full name was Alexandria Troas, and it was situated on the coast of Mysia.

9. ὤφθη τῷ Παύλῳ. The dative of the *agent* is found in classical Greek prose only with the perfect and pluperfect passive.

10. ἐζητήσαμεν. An important verse. The writer here uses for the first time *the first person*. The subsequent narrative, excepting that in chaps. xvii., xviii., xix., contains like proof that the writer was *present* at the events he relates.

— συμβιβάζοντες, *inferring* or *concluding*. See ix. 22. *Putting together* the facts just recorded, that they were not allowed to preach in Asia, nor in Bithynia, and that Paul received an intimation that they should go to Macedonia, *they came to the conclusion* that the Lord had called them to carry the Gospel into Europe.

11. ἀναχθέντες, *having put out to sea*.

11. εὐθυδρομήσαμεν, we made a straight run, we ran before the wind. The voyage was quickly made; it occupied only parts of two days; whereas on the return voyage five days were spent (xx. 6).

— Σαμοθράκην. An island in the Ægæan Sea off the coast of Thrace.

— Νέαν Πόλιν. Neapolis properly belonged to Thrace. It was the port of Philippi, which was about twelve miles inland.

12. Φιλίππους. Founded by Philip of Macedon, and called after his name. It was the scene of the battle between Antony and Octavianus (afterwards Augustus) on the one side, and Brutus and Cassius on the other, in 42 B.C., soon after which it became a Roman Colony.

— ἥτις κ.τ.λ., which is the first Colony-town of the district of Macedonia. Compare Thuc. vi. 62, end.

The difficulty lies in the meaning to be assigned to πρώτη. It may mean the first town reached by them in Macedonia, supposing Neapolis to be reckoned as part of Thrace. It cannot mean the chief city of Macedonia, for that was Amphipolis. But since Amphipolis was not a Roman Colony, it seems best to take πόλις and κολώνια as forming a compound word.

— κολώνια. A Roman Colony was a part of Rome itself removed to the provinces. The inhabitants of the Coloniæ were Roman citizens, still enrolled among the Tribes, and retaining the privilege of voting at Rome. They were governed by their own Senate and Magistrates, and not by the governor of the Province.

13. ποταμόν. A small stream called Gangites.

13. ἐνομίζομεν εἶναι, *we supposed there was*.   But some read ἐνομίζετο εἶναι (προσευχή), *was wont to be*.

— προσευχήν.   The word has three meanings :   (1) prayer, (2) a meeting for prayer, (3) a place in which prayer may be made.   Here the *third* seems preferable.

14. πορφυρόπωλις, *a seller of the purple cloths*.   πορφύρα means (1) the purple-fish ; (2) the purple-dye for wool obtained from the fish ; (3) a purple robe (Mark xv. 17).

— Θυατείρων.   Thyatira, a city of Lydia, was celebrated for the trade of purple dyeing.

— σεβομένη, *one who worshipped*.   She was a Proselyte.

15. ὁ οἶκος αὐτῆς.   From the mention of the baptism of the *household* of Lydia and the *whole family* of the Jailor (verse 33), an argument for the Baptism of Infants is drawn.

— εἰ κεκρίκατε, *if ye have judged*.   εἰ takes the indicative when a *particular* supposition is stated, and the writer expresses *no opinion* as to the fulfilment of the condition.

— παρεβιάσατο, *she pressed us earnestly*.

16. πνεῦμα Πύθωνα (al. Πύθωνος), *a spirit, a Python*. It is hard to determine whether Πύθωνα is here (1) a proper name, in which case it would refer to Apollo, who was worshipped under the name Πύθων at Delphi, or (2) merely equivalent to μαντείαν, *divination*, so that the words mean *a spirit of divination*.

18. ἐποίει, *she continued to do*.

— διαπονηθείς, *being violently distressed* with indignation at the sight.

19. εἵλκυσαν, *dragged.* 1 aor. ἕλκω, fut. ἕλξω, imperf. εἷλκον, aor. εἵλκυσα, perf. εἵλκυκα.

— ἀγοράν. This word should here be rendered *Forum*, as the place was a Colonia.

— τοὺς ἄρχοντας, *the Magistrates;* either the *civil* authorities, who passed them on to the *military* commanders, or put as a general term for those who are specified in the next verse as στρατηγοί.

20. τοῖς στρατηγοῖς, *to the Prætors.* The proper title of these magistrates was *Duumviri* or *Quatuorviri*, as the numbers might vary. Their principal duty was the administration of justice, whence they were called *Duumviri juri dicundo.*

— ἐκταράσσουσιν, *greatly disturb.*

— Ἰουδαῖοι ὑπάρχοντες, *Jews as they are.* An invidious remark put in a stronger light by the antithesis Ῥωμαίοις οὖσι, *Romans as we are.*

22. συνεπέστη, *came suddenly together* with the owners of the damsel. Observe the force which σύν may have in the compound.

— περιρρήξαντες αὐτῶν, *having rent from them,* i.e. from Paul and Silas. περιρρήγνυμι is the regular Attic word for rending garments : see Dem. F. L. 403.

— ἐκέλευον ῥαβδίζειν, *proceeded to give an order to scourge them.* Thucydides uses ἔλεγον and ἐκέλευον in the sense of the *aorist.* See Thuc. vi. 93, and compare Acts xxv. 20.

24. ἠσφαλίσατο, *made fast.*

— τὸ ξύλον, *the stocks.* In Lat. *nervus,* an instrument of wood in which the feet of prisoners were secured.

25. προσευχόμενοι ὕμνουν, *in prayer were praising with*

song. Imperfect ὑμνέω. The participle is used to express any *attendant circumstance.*

25. ἐπηκροῶντο, *were listening to.* Imperfect of ἐπακροάομαι.

26. ἀνεῴχθησαν, *were opened.*

— ἀνέθη, *were loosened.*

27. μάχαιραν, a sword, the first that came to hand.

28. μηδὲν πράξῃς κακόν, *do no harm.* In prohibitory forms with μή, in the second or third persons, the imperative present or the subjunctive aorist may be used.

29. φῶτα, *lights.* Neuter plural.

— ἔντρομος, *full of terror.*

33. ἔλουσεν ἀπὸ τῶν πληγῶν, *he washed (and cleaned them) from their stripes;* that is, from the blood with which they were covered from their stripes.

34. ἀναγαγών, *having led them up.*

— τράπεζαν, *a meal.* τράπεζα, *a table,* is used for that which is set on it (Herod. i. 162; Thuc. i. 130).

35. τοὺς ῥαβδούχους, *the lictors;* so called from carrying (ἔχω) the bundle of rods (ῥάβδοι) before the Prætors.

36. ὅτι introduces the exact words of the speaker.

37. Ῥωμαίους. Roman citizens were exempted from scourging by the Lex Valeria B.C. 500, and the Lex Porcia B.C. 248, which imposed a heavy penalty on any magistrate who should inflict the punishment.

— οὐ γάρ, *why no; nay, indeed.*

— αὐτοί, *in person.* The nominative, whether singular or plural, of αὐτός is always *emphatic.*

40. πρὸς τὴν Λυδίαν, *into the house of Lydia.*

CHAPTER XVII.

1. Amphipolis, so called because it was built conspicuous both towards the sea and towards the land (ἐπ᾽ ἀμφότερα, Thuc. iv. 102), the Strymon flowing round it on both sides, was an Athenian colony ; it subsequently became the chief city of Macedonia Prima.

— Thessalonica, so called by Cassander, who rebuilt it, in honour of his wife Thessalonica, sister of Alexander the Great. It was at this time the chief city of the province of Macedonia, and the residence of the Roman Proconsul. It was made a *free city* (urbs libera) after the battle of Philippi. It is still a flourishing place, called *Saloniki.*

— ἡ συναγωγή. If the article be retained (though the chief MSS. omit it) it probably signifies that at Thessalonica was *the* synagogue of the district, there being none at Philippi, Amphipolis, and Apollonia.

2. κατὰ τὸ εἰωθός, *according to that which was customary.* εἰωθός, perf. part. ἔθω.

— διελέξατο αὐτοῖς, *he argued with them.*

3. διανοίγων καὶ παρατιθέμενος, *opening and setting forth,* i.e. unfolding the hidden truths of Scripture, and applying them to prove his teaching.

— καὶ ὅτι, *and (saying).* Observe the change to the *direct* narration.

— οὗτός ἐστιν, κ.τ.λ., *Jesus, whom I preach to you, is this Messiah.*

4. προσεκληρώθησαν, *were joined.* προσκληρόω, *I as-*

sign by lot, is apparently used with reference to *the decree of God* by which these men were converted.

5. προσλαβόμενοι, *having taken as their assistants.* A common meaning of the word.

— τῶν ἀγοραίων, *of the loiterers in the market.* Used for the idle fellows who lounged about the market-place. Lat. *subrostrani, subbasilicani.*

— ἐπιστάντες, *having made a sudden attack.*

6. ἔσυρον, *they dragged with violence.* See viii. 3.

— τοὺς πολιτάρχας, *the Politarchs.* A title *peculiar*, so far as we know, to the magistrates of Thessalonica. From inscriptions found at Thessalonica we learn that the magistrates of that city, seven in number, were called Πολιτάρχαι.

— οἱ ἀναστατώσαντες, *who have unsettled.* Implying an incitement to sedition. ἀναστατόω is a late word from ἀνάστατος, (1) driven from house and home, (2) engaged in sedition.

7. ὑποδέδεκται, *has received as guests.*

9. λαβόντες τὸ ἱκανόν, *having taken bail.* τὸ ἱκανόν, lit. *that which is satisfactory*, was an expression for *security* or *bail* in late Greek. Lat. *satisdatione accepta.*

10. Berœa, south-west of Thessalonica, in Macedonia Tertia.

— ἀπῄεσαν, *went.* *Compound* verbs in late Greek are often used in the sense of their simple derivatives. Thus here ἀπῄεσαν = ᾔεσαν.

11. εὐγενέστεροι, *more noble-minded, more generous.*

11. οἵτινες, seeing that they; quippe qui. An instance of the explicative force of ὅστις. See ix. 35.

— ἀνακρίνοντες must be taken as the imperfect participle, and the optative ἔχοι follows correctly, the tense used in the direct discourse being retained.

— εἰ ἔχοι ταῦτα οὕτως, (to see) whether these things were so, ἀνακρίνοντες implying that they examined in order to find out.

12. οὖν, so. οὖν is often merely a participle of continuation, but sometimes it also draws an inference from that which precedes; thus here it implies and the result was.

— εὐσχημόνων, of high rank.

13. κἀκεῖ is to be taken with σαλεύοντες, stirring up there also. σαλεύω I make to shake is from σάλος, tossing motion, especially the rolling swell of the sea.

14. ὡς merely marks the purpose of following a certain direction. A subsequent deviation from the direct course is perhaps hinted at. Compare Thuc. v. 3; vi. 61.
Some read ἕως " as far as ".

15. οἱ καθιστάνοντες, they who escorted. καθιστάνω is a late form of καθίστημι, an early meaning of which verb is to bring down, to escort. Hom. Od. xiii. 274; Thuc. iv. 78.

16. τοῦ Παύλου ἐκδεχομένου, as Paul was waiting.

— κατείδωλον, covered with idols. A word of late Greek, formed after the manner of κατάχρυσος, covered with gold; κατάδενδρος, covered with trees.

6

17. οὖν, *so*. Perhaps in consequence of his indignation. See verse 12.

— ἐν τῇ ἀγορᾷ, *in the Agora* or market-place of Athens.

— τοὺς παρατυγχάνοντας, *those who happened to be there.*

18. Epicureans. Followers of Epicurus, a native of Samos, who taught at Athens about 300 B.C. His object was to remove from the minds of men fear of the Gods and dread of death. In his view the world was made by an accidental concourse of atoms. The points of Epicureism which challenged the opposition of St. Paul were these: that there was no Personal Creator, no Moral Governor, no Resurrection of soul or body, and no Judgment to come.

— Stoics. Followers of Zeno of Citium (B.C. 280), who taught at Athens in the painted *portico* (στοά). They were *Pantheists*, regarding God as the Reason of the World, not as the Creator. They believed that the body of man perishes at death, and that his soul is absorbed into the soul of the universe. They taught men to shape all their actions to Reason, the *wise* man only being good and happy.

— συνέβαλλον, *used to converse with.* There is an ellipsis of λόγους. The middle συμβάλλεσθαι is used in this sense by classical writers. Some render *encountered.*

— τί ἂν θέλοι, κ.τ.λ., *what can this babbler wish to say?* The optative with ἄν in an interrogative sentence makes the question more emphatic, *what in the world does he mean?* Compare Il. xix. 90; Od. xxi. 259.

θέλω is frequently used in the phrase τί θέλει; or more fully, τί θέλει λέγειν ;= what does he mean? *quid sibi vult?* Compare Hor. Carm. 3, 8, 2.

18. σπερμολόγος is properly an *adjective, picking up seeds* (σπέρμα, λέγω). Hence ὁ σπερμολόγος as a *noun* was used of *a bird that picks up seed;* thence of *a man who picks up scraps by begging or stealing;* thence of *one who retails scraps of knowledge, an idle babbler.*

19. ἐπιλαβόμενοι, *having laid hold.* The word implies a *gentle* seizure.

— τὸν Ἄρειον πάγον, *the hill of Ares.* So called because Ares, according to tradition, was the first tried there for murder. On it was held the highest judicial court, called the Council of Areopagus.

20. ξενίζοντα, *surprising.* ξενίζω means (1) *I entertain a stranger* (Acts xxi. 16), (2) *I surprise.*

21. Ἀθηναῖοι δὲ πάντες, *now all Athenians.* The omission of the article shows that the Athenians are spoken of in *general* terms as a people.

— εὐκαίρουν, *found leisure.* Imperfect εὐκαιρέω, a word of late Greek.

— καινότερον, *newer than the last news.* But see note on xxv. 10, and compare Thuc. i. 132, νεώτερόν τι ποιεῖν.

22. κατὰ πάντα, *in all respects.*

— ὡς . . . ὑμᾶς θεωρῶ, *I regard you as.*

— δεισιδαιμονεστέρους, *more god-fearing (than other men), unusually god-fearing.* δεισιδαίμων and δεισιδαιμονία (xxv. 19) are words which are used sometimes by way of *censure,* sometimes of *praise.*

23. ἀναθεωρῶν, *examining.*

— σεβάσματα, *objects of worship;* temples, altars, statues.

— ἐπεγέγραπτο, *had been inscribed.*

— ἀγνώστῳ Θεῷ, *to an unknown God.* It seems clear that these were the *very words* of the inscription. We know that the Athenians honoured deities, of whose names and attributes they were ignorant, under the title of ἄγνωστοι θεοί.

— ὃ . . . τοῦτο, *what . . . this* is the true reading.

25. προσδεόμενος, *as if needing,* as one that needs.

— αὐτὸς διδούς, *because He Himself gives.*

— τὰ πάντα, *all things which they have,* or which they need. Observe the force of the article.

26. ἐποίησε, *He made.* Aorist denoting the *single, definite* act of Creation.

— ἐξ ἑνὸς (αἵματος), *from one (blood).* To show that He is the Father of all. The Athenians prided themselves on being earth-born, αὐτόχθονες, and so distinct in lineage from all other men. The reading αἵματος has but little authority.

— κατοικεῖν . . . ζητεῖν. Two objects are assigned for the Creation of men: (1) that they might inhabit the earth; (2) that they might seek the Lord. For the infinitives see Thuc. vi. 93.

— ὁρίσας προτεταγμένους, κ. τ. λ., *having fixed pre-appointed periods and the boundaries of their habitation.* God determined during what time and over what space particular nations should dwell in particular localities.

For προτεταγμένους the best MSS. give προστεταγμένους, *appointed.*

27. εἰ ἄρα γε, *if so be that haply.*

— ψηλαφήσειαν, *they might feel.* From ψηλαφάω, *I feel for, I feel;* used of men who grope after something in the dark. Compare χερσὶ ψηλαφόων, Hom. O. ix. 415.

— καί γε, *although.*

28. ποιητῶν. Aratus, of *Tarsus*, who wrote on Astronomy about 270 B.C., and Cleanthes, a Lycian, are referred to.

— τοῦ γὰρ καὶ γένος ἐσμέν. The commencement of a hexameter.

St. Paul quotes a verse from Greek poetry in two other passages :—

(1) Tit. i. 12. Κρῆτες ἀεὶ ψεῦσται, κακὰ θηρία, γαστέρες ἀργαί (Epimenides).

(2) 1 Cor. xv. 33. φθείρουσιν ἤθη χρῆσθ᾽ ὁμιλίαι κακαί (Menander).

29. νομίζειν τὸ θεῖον εἶναι ὅμοιον χρυσῷ. Such is the order of construction, *to think that that which is divine is like gold,* &c.

— χαράγματι, κ. τ. λ., *the graving of the art and the device of man,*

τέχνης refers to the *manual* skill; ἐνθυμήσεως to the *mental* conception of the sculptor.

30. ὑπεριδών, *having overlooked, i.e.* having graciously abstained from punishing.

31. ἐν δικαιοσύνῃ, *in righteousness.* Dat. to denote the *element* in which the judgment will take place.

— ἐν ἀνδρί, *by the Man.*

— ᾧ ὥρισε, *whom He appointed.* ᾧ for ὅν by attraction.

34. ὁ ᾿Αρεοπαγίτης, *a member of the Council of Areopagus.* See verse 19.

Dionysius according to tradition was Bishop of Athens, and suffered martyrdom.

— γυνή. Some render it *his wife*, without any ground.

CHAPTER XVIII.

1. χωρισθείς, *having departed.* 1 aor. passive with a *middle* signification.

— Κόρινθον. Corinth was at this time the capital of the province of Achaia, and the residence of the Proconsul.

2. Aquila and Priscilla were with St. Paul at Ephesus (1 Cor. xvi. 19) ; they subsequently went to Rome (Rom. xvi. 3), and we hear of them again at Ephesus (2 Tim. iv. 19).

— προσφάτως, *recently.* From πρόσφατος, *fresh*, a word which originally meant *lately slain.*

— διατεταχέναι, *had issued an edict.*

— Κλαύδιον. Suetonius in his life of Claudius tells us that that Emperor expelled the Jews from Rome because they were continually exciting tumults, *impulsore Chresto*, which probably refers to the name, real or assumed, of the person who was the leader in the disturbances.

3. εἰργάζετο, *used to work.* Compare especially Acts xx. 34, and 1 Cor. iv. 12.

It was customary among the Jews to teach the children even of the richer class some trade.

5. Μακεδονίας. We learn from 2 Cor. xi. 9, that the Macedonian Christians sent pecuniary aid to St. Paul. " *That which was lacking to me the brethren which came from Macedonia supplied.*"

— συνείχετο τῷ λόγῳ, *was anxiously occupied with teaching;* or it may mean, *was constrained by the word* within him, urging him to preach.

The reading of the received text, πνεύματι, has no authority. With it the meaning would be, *was constrained in his spirit,* or, *was constrained by the Holy Spirit.*

— συνέχομαι means, *I am hard pressed, I am worried,* followed by the dative of that which causes the distress. See especially Herod. iii. 131.

— διαμαρτυρόμενος, *solemnly testifying; sanctissime affirmans.*

6. ἐκτιναξάμενος, *having shaken out.* Shaking off the dust was a symbolic action to mark abhorrence at abominable conduct. Compare xiii. 51.

— τὸ αἷμα ὑμῶν. Ellipsis of ἐλθέτω. See Matt. xxiii. 35.

7. ἐκεῖθεν, *from that building,* i.e. the synagogue.

— συνομοροῦσα, *contiguous.*

10. τοῦ κακῶσαι, *for the purpose of maltreating.* Genitive of *design.*

11. ἐκάθισε, *he settled, i.e.* made Corinth his permanent abode.

12. Gallio was brother of Seneca the philosopher, and uncle of Lucan the poet. He was a man of very amiable disposition. When he heard of the death of Seneca he committed suicide.

— ἀνθυπάτου ὄντος, *being Proconsul.* We know that Achaia was a *Senatorial* Province at the time. It had been an *Imperial* Province under Tiberius, but Claudius restored it to the Senate. See note on xiii. 7.

— Achaia as a province contained the whole of Proper Greece, including the Peloponnesus. The Province of Macedonia included Macedonia, Illyria, Epirus, and Thessaly.

13. τὸ βῆμα, *the tribunal,* a raised seat on which the Proconsul sat when matters were brought before him for trial.

14. οὖν. If this word be retained it must be rendered *now* or *so,* the words of Gallio being a *continuation* of previous remarks, or an *answer* to the complaints of the Jews. But probably it should be omitted.

— ῥᾳδιούργημα, *an act of villany :* more criminal than ἀδίκημα, *an act of wrong.*

— κατὰ λόγον, *with reason.*

— περὶ λόγου, *about doctrine.*

15. τοῦ καθ᾿ ὑμᾶς, *that prevails among you.*

15. ὄψεσθε αὐτοί, *ye shall look to it yourselves.* Observe the future.

— βούλομαι, *I wish,* expresses a positive inclination ; θέλω, *I am willing,* simply means, *I make no objection.* Such is the *A*ttic usage.

16. ἀπήλασεν, *he drove.*

17. πάντες. Probably *all the mob.* Some add οἱ "Ελληνες, others οἱ 'Ιουδαῖοι : with the latter reading we must suppose that the Jews beat Sosthenes because he was converted by St. Paul.

18. ἀποταξάμενος, *having bidden farewell,* a meaning not found in classical Greek. It seems to come from the notion of giving *final* directions.

— κειράμενος, *having shorn.* It is not certain whether this refers to St. Paul or to Aquila. Probably to St. Paul. If the vow by which the Apostle was bound were the vow of the Nazarite (which seems not unlikely from xxi. 24), we must take the following explanation : a Nazarite was bound to let his hair grow till the expiration of his vow, and then he had *to shave* (ξυράω) his head ; but if he were in a *foreign* land he might *poll* (κείρω) his hair, and carry it to Jerusalem to be offered in the Temple.

— Κεγχρεαῖς. *Cenchreœ,* on the Saronic Gulf, was one of the two ports of Corinth, the other being *Lechæum,* on the Corinthian Gulf.

21. ἀνήχθη. κατελθών. ἀναβάς. κατέβη. A good illustration of the uses of ἀνά and κατά with verbs of motion is to be observed in this and the following verse :

when you *leave* the coast-line, either to put out to sea or to go up into the country, ἀνά is used; when you *go towards* the coast-line, either from the open sea or from the interior of the country, κατά is used.

23. καθεξῆς, *one after another, in order.*

24. Ἀπολλώς. A contraction of Ἀπολλώνιος. Modern criticism inclines to favour the suggestion, first made by Luther, that Apollos wrote the Epistle to the Hebrews.

— λόγιος may mean *erudite* or *eloquent*, probably the latter.

25. κατηχημένος, *instructed.* The meanings of κατηχέω are:

(1) I sound.
(2) I give oral instruction, *viva voce doceo.*
(3) I instruct in the *rudiments* of some subject.

In the New Testament, *rudimentary* instruction is generally hinted at.

— ζέων, *being fervent.* Partic. of ζέω, *I boil with heat* or *passion.*

— ἀκριβῶς, *accurately.*

26. προσελάβοντο αὐτόν, *took him to their own house.*

27. προτρεψάμενοι ἔγραψαν, *wrote recommending.* The participle is used to express any *attendant circumstance*, as in xvi. 25. Observe that the tense of the participle is adapted to the tense of the verb. The Revised Version has *encouraged him and wrote.* See note on xxv. 13.

— συνεβάλετο, *assisted.* A meaning which the *middle* of συμβάλλω has.

27. τοῖς πεπιστευκόσι διὰ τῆς χάριτος, *those who had believed through grace*, *i.e.* whom the grace of God had made believers.

Some take συνεβάλετο διὰ τῆς χάριτος together, *assisted through grace*.

28. εὐτόνως, *forcibly*. Adv. of εὔτονος, *sinewy, nervous*. See Ar. Plut. 1095.

— διακατηλέγχετο, *he thoroughly confuted in argument*. The simple verb ἐλέγχω means *I convince another that he is in the wrong*.

CHAPTER XIX.

1. Ἀπολλώ for Ἀπολλών, the regular acc. sing. of Ἀπολλώς—ών—ώ—ῴ.

— τὰ ἀνωτερικὰ μέρη, *the inland parts*. Lit. *the up-country districts*. Perhaps Phrygia and Galatia.

—Ἔφεσον. The capital of the Roman province of Asia, in the district of Ionia, about the middle of the western coast of the peninsula commonly called Asia Minor.

2. εἰ ἐλάβετε ; *did ye receive?* εἰ was a regular interrogative particle in late Greek. See i. 6.

— πιστεύσαντες, *when ye believed*, *i.e.* at the time when ye were admitted to be members of the Church after a profession of your belief. The participle often expresses circumstances of *time*.

— ἀλλά, *so far from that*.

— οὐδὲ ἠκούσαμεν, *we did not even hear*.

2. εἰ Πνεῦμα Ἅγιον ἔστιν, *whether there is a Holy Spirit*. ἔστιν is here *emphatic*, implying that they had not heard of the existence of the Holy Spirit. A less probable explanation is that they had not heard·that a reception of the Holy Spirit is essential for the full enjoyment of the privileges connected with Christian Baptism. Compare Joh. vii. 39.

3. The only requisite for John's Baptism was *Repentance*: Christian Baptism required *Faith*, was performed in the Name of the Trinity, and was followed by Grace.

4. ἐβάπτισε βάπτισμα, *baptized with a baptism*. Cognate accusative.

— μετάνοια and μεταμέλεια differ in this way: the former means *a change of mind*, the latter *a change of purpose*. μετάνοια is used to express a change of opinion when it *first commences*; μεταμέλεια implies that the change of opinion *continues* (Thuc. iii. 36, 37). In the New Testament the former only occurs.

5. εἰς τὸ ὄνομα, *into the name*. See note on viii. 16.

6. ἐπιθέντος. The *second* instance of Confirmation. See viii. 17.

7. οἱ πάντες, *in all*. The article is used with πᾶς in definitions of number (xxvii. 37).

8. πείθων τὰ περί, *teaching persuasively the things concerning*. πείθω is followed by two accusatives. It is sometimes found with the accusative of the thing taught only, as in Soph. Œd. Col. 1442.

9. τὴν ὁδόν, *the Way*, *i.e.* the religion. See ix. 2.

— ἀφώρισε, *he withdrew*.

9. σχολῇ, *school.* The word σχολή meant (1) *leisure*; (2) that in which leisure is employed, especially *a learned discussion*; (3) the place where such discussions or lectures were held, *a school.*

11. οὐ τὰς τυχούσας, *of no ordinary kind.* Compare especially xxviii. 2. ·

The phrase ὁ τυχών, Lat *quivis, the first one meets, a common man,* is of frequent occurrence.

12. χρωτός, *person.* χρώς means strictly *the skin,* but it is also used for *the body.*

— σουδάρια, *handkerchiefs.* From the Lat. *sudarium.*

— σιμικίνθια, *aprons.* From the Lat. *semicinctium,* an apron used by mechanics.

13. ἐξορκιστῶν. From a remarkable passage of Josephus (Ant. viii. 2, 5) we learn that Jews of his day did, according to his view, actually drive out demons from men by means of a method of exorcism discovered by Solomon. See also Matt. xii. 27.

— ὁρκίζομεν ὑμᾶς τὸν Ἰησοῦν, *we adjure you by Jesus.* ὁρκίζω, a form of ὁρκόω, takes two accusatives.

14. ἀρχιερέως, *a chief-priest.* Probably one of the heads of the twenty-four priestly families.

16. κατακυριεύσας ἀμφοτέρων, *having mastered both of them.* The true reading is ἀμφοτέρων instead of αὐτῶν, *two only* being engaged in the work at the time.

18. ἀναγγέλλοντες, κ.τ.λ., *describing their methods of proceeding.*

19. τὰ περίεργα, *curious arts, magic.* The word περίεργος is used in an *active* sense as (1) *over-careful,* (2) *a*

busy-body ; and in a *passive* sense as (1) *over-wrought,*
elaborate, (2) *superfluous.*

19. τὰς βίβλους, *their books,* containing the formulæ
used in incantations. Compare Dem. F. L. 221.

— μυριάδας. Substantive ; *ten thousands.* Render
fifty thousand pieces of silver, ἀργυρίου being put for
δραχμῶν. Compare Thuc. v. 63.

The Attic drachma $= 9\frac{1}{4}d.$; the drachma at this time
was the same as the Roman denarius $= 8d.$

20. κατὰ κράτος, *mightily,* like κατὰ φύσιν, *naturally.*

21. ἔθετο, *purposed ;* lit. *fixed, placed firmly.*

22. ἐπέσχε χρόνον, *he stopped.* The phrase is classical,
Thuc. iv. 73.

— εἰς τὴν 'Ασίαν, *with the intention of visiting Asia.*
The preposition is difficult to explain.

23. περὶ τῆς ὁδοῦ, *with respect to the Way,* i.e. the religion. Comp. ix. 2.

24. ἀργυροκόπος (ἄργυρος, κόπτω), *a beater of silver, a*
silversmith.

— ναοὺς ἀργυροῦς 'Αρτέμιδος, *silver models of the temple*
of Artemis. Small portable models carried away by the
worshippers.

— τεχνίταις, *craftsmen,* skilled workmen or designers.

25. τοὺς ἐργάτας, *those who were employed,* perhaps less
skilful than the τεχνῖται.

— περὶ τὰ τοιαῦτα, *about such matters,* memorials of
the Temple. The article gives a *demonstrative* force,
such things as have been just named, i.e. ναοὺς ἀργυροῦς.

26. πάσης τῆς 'Ασίας, *throughout the whole of Asia.* The genitive of *place* is rarely found in *prose.* But see Plat. Symp. 182; Thuc. v. 33.

— μετέστησε, *perverted,* drew away from the worship of the Gods.

27. *And not only is this employment in danger of coming into disrepute to our loss, but also (there is danger) of the temple of the great goddess Artemis being made of no account, and also (there is danger) that there is about to be a destruction of the magnificence of her, whom the whole of Asia and the inhabited world venerate.*

— ἡμῖν, *to our loss.* Dative of *reference,* or *dativus incommodi.*

— μέρος, *part, department,* is here used in the sense of *employment.*

28. Ἄρτεμις. The Temple at Ephesus having been burnt to the ground on the night on which Alexander the Great was born (355 B.C.), was restored with increased magnificence, and was regarded as one of the wonders of the world. The Ephesian Artemis was probably distinct from the Greek Artemis, the huntress-goddess, the Diana of the Romans. She was called the "Goddess of the many breasts," πολύμαστος, *multi-mammia,* a mode of representation symbolizing the productive and nutritive powers of nature.

30. οὐκ εἴων, *would not allow.* Imperfect ἐάω. The imperfect often expresses attempted action.

31. 'Ασιαρχῶν, *Asiarchs.* Deputies appointed to preside over the games which were held at Ephesus in the month of May in honour of Artemis.

31. δοῦναι, *to hazard.* The word implies *a risk.*

33. Ἀλέξανδρον. About this person nothing is known. He may have been put forward by his countrymen to speak in their behalf; or, being a Christian, he was pushed forward by the Jews to be the victim of the fury of the mob. The Jews thrust him forward (προβαλόντων) into the crowd, the crowd pushed him out to the front (συνεβίβασαν). This meaning *pushed out* for συμβιβάζω is unusual. Some read προεβίβασαν, *pushed forward.*

— κατασείσας τὴν χεῖρα, *waving his hand to obtain silence.* The *accusative* seems to be used because he *continued* doing it without avail: in the other passages in which κατασείω is used in the Acts (xii. 17, xiii. 16, xxi. 40) it is followed by the *dative* τῇ χειρί, because silence was *obtained.*

34. Notice the *anakoluthon* ἐπιγνόντες . . . φωνή, κ. τ. λ., where we might have expected ἐφώνησαν ἅπαντες.

35. ὁ γραμματεύς, *the town-clerk.* An officer who kept the archives of the State, and who read documents of importance in the public assemblies. He combined the duties of a Registrary and a Public Orator.

— γάρ adds *emphasis* to the question, as in viii. 31 ; or it introduces one of *the grounds* on which the speaker makes his appeal, the other being given in 37.

— νεωκόρον, *warden of the Temple* (νεώς, *a temple,* and κορέω, *I sweep*); a title of honour claimed and cherished by the city of Ephesus. All the cities of Asia assisted in building the Temple; Ephesus was honoured with the care of it. Compare Xen. An. v. 3, 6.

— τοῦ διοπετοῦς, *of the image that fell from heaven.*

The subst. ἀγάλματος may be supplied, or τὸ διοπετές may be taken for *that which fell from heaven*. This image was a rude block of wood fashioned in the upper part into the semblance of a woman covered with breasts.

37. ἱεροσύλους, *robbers of temples*, hence, as here, *sacrilegious persons*.

38. ἀγοραῖοι (ἡμέραι), *the court-days*, i.e. assizes. ἀγόραιοι, *idlers in the market* (xvii. 5), has a *different* accent, but the Grammarians differ as to the accent assigned to each.

— ἀνθύπατοι, *proconsuls*. Either the *generic* plural put for the singular, or perhaps including the governors of other states of Asia who were at Ephesus at the time, and who would assist *the* Proconsul in hearing causes.

— ἐγκαλείτωσαν, *let them prosecute*.

40. κινδυνεύομεν ἐγκαλεῖσθαι, *are in danger of being prosecuted*.

— στάσεως, *disturbance*. συστροφῆς, *confusion*.

CHAPTER XX.

1. ἀσπασάμενος, *having saluted them* with the kiss of *departure*. This is the *proper* word, for which ἀποταξάμενος is put in xviii. 18.

2. μέρη, *districts*. αὐτούς, *the inhabitants*, the Macedonian Christians.

It seems likely that St. Paul went as far as *Illyricum* at this time (Rom. xv. 19).

— Ἑλλάδα. Southern Greece, the province of Achaia.

7

3. ποιήσας, *having spent.*

— ἐγένετο γνώμης *he formed a determination.*

4. Ἀσιανοί, *natives of Asia.* Distinguish it from Ἀσιαρχαί (xix. 31).

5. ἡμᾶς. Hence we conclude that no one of the persons mentioned in verse 4 was the author of this work. This is important, because some have ascribed the authorship of the book to Timothy.

7. τῇ μιᾷ τῶν σαββάτων, *the first day of the week.* The origin of the phrase seems to have been the Hebrew usage of speaking of the days of the week as *one after the Sabbath, two after the Sabbath.* In this verse we have the first distinct allusion to a meeting of the Christians on the first day of the week for a religious service, for John xx. 19 scarcely goes so far as this. We may *infer* from the New Testament that the Lord's Day was regularly observed, but it is not till the second century that we find the practice *clearly* described and directly associated with our Lord's Resurrection on that day.

— τοῦ κλάσαι ἄρτον, *for the purpose of breaking bread,* possibly referring to the celebration of the Holy Eucharist. But it may refer to the common meal, as in ii. 42.

8. λαμπάδες, *torches.*

9. θυρίδος, *window-sill.* The window of an Oriental house consists still of an aperture closed in with lattice-work. When the lattice-work was open, there was nothing to prevent a person from falling through the aperture. See 2 Kings i. 2.

— καταφερόμενος, *being weighed down,* gradually and increasingly (*present*).

9. κατενεχθείς, *having been overpowered*, suddenly and completely (*aorist*).

— ἐπὶ πλεῖον, *yet further*, or perhaps, *to an unusual extent*, *i.e.* longer than was his wont.   The phrase occurs in iv. 17 and xxiv. 4.

— ἀπὸ τοῦ ὕπνου, *in consequence of the sleep*.   ἀπό is used for the *cause* or *occasion* (compare xi. 19), where we might expect ὑπό, in a few passages in classical authors, the preposition having then a mixed notion of *derivation* and *agency* (Thuc. i. 17 ; iv. 115).   A great modern critic regards all such passages as corrupt.

The article is prefixed to ὕπνου because this sleep was mentioned before in ὕπνῳ βαθεῖ.

— τριστέγου (οἰκήματος), *a chamber on the third story*, τρίστεγος being an adjective.

— κάτω, *down*, put at the end for emphasis.   Compare Herod. iii. 75, and Aristoph. Ran. 130—133, which reads like a parody on the passage in Herodotus.

10. ἐπέπεσεν.   So did Elijah (1 Kings xvii. 21), and Elisha (2 Kings iv. 34).

11. κλάσας ἄρτον.   The probable reading is τὸν ἄρτον, *the* bread mentioned in verse 7.

— ὁμιλήσας, *having talked with them*.

— οὕτως, *thereupon*.

13. ἀνήχθημεν, κ. τ. λ., *put out to sea for Assus*, in Mysia, opposite the island Lesbos.

— ἦν διατεταγμένος, *he had appointed*. Perf. pass. in a *middle* sense.

— πεζεύειν, *to go by land*.

14. Mitylene was the chief city of the island Lesbos, on the eastern coast.

15. ἄντικρυς. Adverb, *over against, opposite.*

— Chios, an island off the coast of Ionia, just north of the bay of Ephesus.

— παρεβάλομεν, *we put in,* or, *we put across to.* The word is so used in Thuc. iii. 32.

— Samos, now *Scio*, an island just south of the bay of Ephesus.

— Trogyllium, a promontory in Ionia, the southern extremity of the bay of Ephesus.

— Miletus, an important town, once the capital of Ionia.

16. παραπλεῦσαι, *to sail by.* Miletus was about forty miles from Ephesus.

— ὅπως μὴ γένηται αὐτῷ, *that it might not happen to him,* or, *that circumstances might not compel him.*

— εἰ δυνατὸν εἴη. The *optative* is used because doubt as to the fulfilment of the condition is implied. See xvi. 15. If no opinion as to his ability to proceed had been expressed, the *indicative* (ἦν) would have been used, as in xxvii. 39.

— γενέσθαι, *should be (spent by him).*

18. ἀφ' ἧς, *from which = on which.* For the use of ἀπό to denote the *commencement of a period*, see xv. 7.

19. πάσης ταπεινοφροσύνης, *every kind of humility.*

— πειρασμῶν, *trials.* Compare Gal. iv. 14.

20. οὐδὲν ὑπεστειλάμην τῶν συμφερόντων, I kept back nothing of the things that were beneficial. Or οὐδέν may be used adverbially, in no way, the sentence being rendered I kept back in no way from things that were beneficial. Dem. F. L. 390.

— τοῦ μὴ ἀναγγεῖλαι, so that I should not announce. Genitive of design (see xv. 20, and Thuc. viii. 14), or it may depend upon ὑπεστειλάμην, being put to explain more definitely the expression τῶν συμφερόντων.

— κατ᾽ οἴκους, from house to house.

22. δεδεμένος τῷ πνεύματι, constrained in my spirit.

23. κατὰ πόλιν, in every city.

— δεσμά. Neuter plural from the masculine sing. δεσμός.

24. ὡς τελειῶσαι, in order that I may finish. The only passage in the New Testament in which ὡς before the infinitive occurs. It may be taken thus: provided that I may finish, ὡς being put for ὥστε = ed conditione ut. ὡς is sometimes used with the infinitive instead of ὥστε, generally to express a result, but seldom (as here) to express a purpose. But probably we should read ὡς τελειώσω.

— καὶ τὴν διακονίαν, even the ministration.

— τῆς χάριτος. Genitive of import or contents. The grace of God is the import, that which is contained in and revealed by the Gospel. Compare 1 Tim. i. 11.

25. οὐκέτι. There is reason to suppose that St. Paul did visit Ephesus again, after his first imprisonment.

26. μαρτύρομαι ὑμῖν, I protest to you.

27. οὐ γὰρ ὑπεστειλάμην τοῦ μὴ ἀναγγεῖλαι, *for I did not flinch from announcing.* The genitive here seems clearly to depend on ὑπεστειλάμην. For μή we might expect μὴ οὐ, but occasionally οὐ is omitted in classical writers. Soph. Ant. 443.

28. ἐπισκόπους, *overseers.* A word pointing to the *duties of* the office, whereas πρεσβύτερος refers rather to the *personal qualifications for* the office. See xi. 30.

— ποιμαίνειν, *to tend.* A word "involving the whole office of the shepherd, the entire leading, guiding, guarding, folding of the flock, as well as the finding of nourishment for it" (Trench, Syn. 98). For the construction see xii. 4.

— Θεοῦ. A strong assertion of the divinity of Christ. Another reading is Κυρίου, which is preferred by the best modern critics. The Alexandrian MS. has Κυρίου; the Vatican MS. Θεοῦ; the Codex Sinaiticus, Θεοῦ.

— περιεποιήσατο, *acquired for himself.* See 1 Tim. iii. 13, and Thuc. i. 9 and 15.

29. ἄφιξιν, *departure.* An unusual sense of the word.

30. διεστραμμένα, *perverted things.*
False teachers did arise in Ephesus (see 1 Tim. i. 20, and 2 Tim. ii. 17), by name Alexander, Hymenæus, and Philetus; the two latter taught that "the resurrection was already past".

32. τῷ δυναμένῳ may refer to Θεῷ, *who is able,* or to λόγῳ, *which is able.*

33. ἱματισμοῦ. Fine raiment formed an important part of the wealth of Orientals. Compare 2 Kings v. 22,

and the expression "where *moth* and rust doth corrupt" (Matt. vi. 19).

33. ἐπεθύμησα, *I coveted, i.e.* when he was at Ephesus.

35. πάντα, *in all respects.*

— οὕτω, *so,* as I laboured.

— κοπιῶντας, *labouring.* In classical Greek κοπιάω means *I am weary;* in later Greek *I work hard.*

— ἀντιλαμβάνεσθαι means (1) *to take hold of,* (2) *to assist,* as here. Thuc. ii. 61.

— τῶν ἀσθενούντων, *the weak,* meaning *the poor.*

— μακάριον, κ. τ. λ. A saying of our Lord not recorded in the Gospels.

37. κατεφίλουν, *they kissed affectionately.* Lat. *deosculabantur.*

38. θεωρεῖν, *to gaze upon.* Stronger than ὄπτομαι in verse 25.

CHAPTER XXI.

1. ὡς δὲ ἐγένετο, *when it came about.*

— ἀποσπασθέντας, *having torn ourselves away.* The word expresses *reluctance to part.*

— Cos, an island opposite Cnidus in Caria, famous for wine and rich stuffs.

— Κῶ, an irregular form of Κῶν, the regular accusative, is the reading of the best MSS. Compare xix. i.

— Rhodes, a large island, south-east of Cos, off the west coast of Lycia.

1. Patara, in Lycia, famous for an oracle of Apollo.

2. διαπερῶν, *crossing over*, by a direct course.

— ἀναφανέντες Κύπρον, *having sighted Cyprus.* When a verb governing two cases, one of a *person*, the other of a *thing*, is used in the passive, the noun denoting the *person* becomes the nominative.

3. εὐώνυμον, *on the left.* The word originally meant *of good name, of good omen ;* and since *bad omens* came from the left, and the Greeks spoke of bad influences by *euphemistic* titles, they used εὐώνυμος in speaking of the left hand.

— Tyre, in Phœnicia, north-west of Palestine. It was still a place of some importance.

— ἐκεῖσε is properly *thither, to that place*, and it may be so here, *thither the ship was bound to discharge her freight.* But it may be put for ἐκεῖ, *there*, as in Thuc. vi. 77.

— ἦν ἀποφορτιζόμενον. Lit. *was discharging*, here put for *was going to discharge.* This use of the part. present with εἶναι instead of the finite verb is common in the New Testament. Compare viii. 28 and xxi. 29.

4. ἀνευρόντες, *having made out, having discovered.*

5. ἐξαρτίσαι, *had completed.* ἐξαρτίζω, a word of late Greek, means *I refit* a ship, or, as here, *I complete.* The aor. is used for the pluperf. inf. See xiii. 29.

6. εἰς τὰ ἴδια, *to their own homes.*

7. Ptolemais, anciently called Accho, and now St. Jean d'Acre.

8. τοῦ εὐαγγελιστοῦ. Evangelist, used of one who went about preaching the Gospel, was much the same in meaning as Missionary now is. See 2 Tim. iv. 5.

— τοῦ ὄντος, *who was.* The article is omitted in the best MSS., in which case the meaning may be *because he was one of the Seven,* giving *the reason* for St. Paul going to his house; or, erasing the comma after εὐαγγελιστοῦ, *who was* the *Evangelist from among the Seven, i.e.* who was the one of the Seven Deacons who went about as an Evangelist.

10. Ἄγαβος. Perhaps the same person who is mentioned in xi. 28.

11. αὐτοῦ, *Paul's;* but ἑαυτοῦ, *his own,* is the correct reading.

For similar symbolical actions to make predictions more impressive, compare 1 Kings xxii. 11; 2 Kings xiii. 15; Jer. xiii. 1—11.

12. οἱ ἐντόπιοι, *the residents, i.e.* the *Christians* of the place.

— τοῦ μὴ ἀναβαίνειν. For the construction see xv. 20.

13. τί ποιεῖτε; *what do ye?* i.e. what is your motive? Comp. Mark. xi. 5.

— εἰς Ἱερουσαλήμ, (*when I shall have come*) *to Jerusalem.*

— ἑτοίμως ἔχω, *I am ready.* This use of ἔχω with adverbs of *manner* is very common; thus καλῶς ἔχειν, *to be prosperous.* Compare Mark v. 23.

15. ἀποσκευασάμενοι, *having packed up our baggage.*

From ἀποσκευάζω, *I pack and carry away;* but as it is said that the verb can only mean *I put down part of my baggage,* it seems better to take the other reading, ἐπισκευασάμενοι, meaning *having equipped ourselves.*

The Authorised Version has *we took up our carriages;* in old English, *carriages* meant *things carried, baggage.* So in Judg. xviii. 21, *carriage* is put for *baggage.*

16. Μνάσωνι, κ. τ. λ. The last five words of the verse are in the *dative,* instead of the *accusative,* by *inverse attraction* with ᾧ; *bringing one Mnason . . . with whom;* or Μνάσωνι is put by attraction for παρὰ Μνάσωνα, *bringing us to Mnason . . . with whom.*

18. πρὸς Ἰάκωβον, *to the house of James,* head of the Church at Jerusalem. See xii. 17.

19. καθ᾽ ἕν, *separately, one by one.*

20. μυριάδες, *tens of thousands.*

— ζηλωταί, *ardent supporters.*

21. κατηχήθησαν, *they were imformed,* aorist. See xviii. 25.

— διδάσκεις. Followed by *two* accusatives, ἀποστασίαν and τοὺς Ἰουδαίους.

— τοῖς ἔθεσι, *in the customs.* Dative of *rule* or *custom,* as in xv. 1.

22. πάντως, *beyond all doubt.* πλῆθος, *a crowd.*

23. ἡμῖν, *among us. Local* dative.

— ἐφ᾽ ἑαυτῶν, *on themselves,* or *perhaps (made) for themselves;* for ἐφ᾽ ἑαυτοῦ = *suâ sponte* in classical Greek.

24. παραλαβών, *having taken to thyself, i.e.* as thy companions.

24. ἁγνίσθητι, *become consecrated.* ἁγνίζω is the word used in the Septuagint for the act of consecration by which the Nazarite bound himself to abstain from wine and strong drink, from cutting his hair, and from touching a dead body.

— δαπάνησον, *spend money.* It was customary for wealthy Jews to assist poor Nazarites in buying the sacrifices which they had to offer. For the sacrifices to be offered, see Numb. vi.

— ξυρήσωνται, *they may shave.* A Nazarite shaved his head *at the completion of his vow,* and offered the hair on the Altar of Sacrifice. The expression "that they may shave their heads" is equivalent to saying, "that they may complete their vow".

Some read ξυρήσονται, the fut. indic. put for vividness, as in v. 15. In classical Greek ὅπως, but not ἵνα, is thus used.

— ὅτι ὧν, κ. τ. λ., *that no one of the things which* (ὧν = τούτων ἅ) *they have been taught concerning thee is true.*

— στοιχεῖς, *walk in orderly fashion,* as a soldier when marching to battle.

25. ἐπεστείλαμεν, *sent written directions.*

— φυλάσσεσθαι αὐτούς, *that they should shun.* φυλάσσω, *I guard,* as in verse 24; φυλάσσομαι, *I am on my guard against.*

26. ἁγνισθείς, *being consecrated,* i.e. having taken the vow of the Nazarite.

— διαγγέλλων τὴν ἐκπλήρωσιν, *announcing the fulfilment,* i.e. taking upon himself the responsibility of seeing that the party performed the vow duly to the end.

26. ἕως οὗ προσηνέχθη, κ. τ. λ., *till the offering was offered*. ἕως with aor. ind. usually denotes a definite event in *past* time. Perhaps the indicative is used here because the action is regarded by the writer as *virtually* completed, in consequence of the promise made by St. Paul to the officiating priest.

The subjunctive is used with ἕως οὗ in xxiii. 14, where an intention not carried into effect is described.

27. αἱ ἑπτὰ ἡμέραι, *the* seven days. No mention is made in the Old Testament of the duration of the period of the vow of the Nazarite. *Thirty* days appears to have been the usual period. Bishop Wordsworth's suggestion, that the seven days may refer to the time between the notice given to the Priest and the end of the vow, seems reasonable.

— συνέχεον, *stirred up*. Imperf. συγχέω = *valde perturbo*.

28. τόπου τούτου, *this Place*, the Temple.

— εἰσήγαγεν, *he brought in*. Aorist, on one particular occasion.

— κεκοίνωκε, *he hath defiled*. Perfect, marking the *continuance* of the pollution.

29. ἦσαν προεωρακότες, *they had previously seen*, or, as Meyer takes it, *they had seen from afar*, a classical use of the verb (Thuc. viii. 44). Instances of this resolution of the verb into the participle with εἶναι, *to give force to the predicate*, may be found in Æsch. Ag. 1178 ; Thuc. iii. 97.

30. ἔξω τοῦ ἱεροῦ. That they might not pollute the Temple with blood.

31. ἀνέβη φάσις, *information went up* to Fort Antonia, which stood close to the north-western corner of the Temple. It was built by Herod the Great, and was called Antonia in honour of Antonius the triumvir.

— τῷ χιλιάρχῳ τῆς σπείρης, *to the Tribune of the Cohort.* The legion contained 6100 infantry, divided into 10 cohorts, each containing 6 centuries. Each legion was commanded by a Legatus, each cohort by a Tribune, each century by a Centurion.

33. ἀλύσεσι δυσί. So that he was bound to a soldier on each side. See xii. 6.

— τίσ εἴη, *who he might be.*

— τί ἐστι πεποιηκώς, *what he had done.* The indicative marks the second question as of more importance than the first. Compare Xen. Cyr. iv. 4, 4.

34. τὸ ἀσφαλές, *the certain truth.*

— παρεμβολήν, *fort.* The word is used in late Greek for *an entrenched camp;* here it is applied to the barracks of the soldiers in Fort Antonia.

35. ἀναβαθμούς, *steps,* leading from the Temple to the Fort.

— συνέβη, κ. τ. λ., *it fell out that he was taken off his feet.* See note on xi. 26.

36. αἶρε αὐτόν, *away with him, i.e. kill him.*

37. Ἑλληνιστί γινώσκεις ; *do you understand Greek?* See xiv. 11.

38. οὐκ ἄρα σὺ εἶ ; *art thou not then?* implying that the Tribune thought Paul *was* the Egyptian, who shortly

before this collected a large body of followers, and was routed by Felix the Procurator.

38. τετρακισχιλίους. Josephus says the Egyptian brought thirty thousand men *to* Jerusalem; St. Luke says he led *out* four thousand men : there is no contradiction, but it may be observed that Josephus deals very freely with numbers.

— σικαρίων, *assassins.* From the Latin word *sicarius,* a cut-throat, from *sica,* a dagger. Josephus tells us that Jerusalem was at this time infested by a set of ruffians called Sicarii, who frequently stabbed men with their daggers.

40. κατέσεισε, κ. τ. λ., *motioned the people to silence with his hand.* See xii. 17.

— Ἑβραΐδι. He spoke in the Aramaic language.

CHAPTER XXII.

1. ἄνδρες, omitted in English. *Brethren and Fathers.*

3. πόδας. Jewish scholars sat, the younger on the ground, the elder on benches, to hear their teachers, who delivered their lectures from an elevated seat.

— κατὰ ἀκρίβειαν, *according to the strict accuracy.*

— ζηλωτὴς τοῦ Θεοῦ, *zealous in the cause of God.*

4. ταύτην τὴν ὁδόν, *this way,* i.e. Christianity. See viii. 3.

— ἄχρι θανάτου, *unto death;* implying that he did all in his power to do away with Christianity.

5. ὁ ἀρχιερεύς. The high-priest of *that* time, *Theophilus*, who was still living. The high-priest at the time when this speech was made was *Ananias* (xxiii. 2).

— τὸ πρεσβυτήριον, *the College of Elders;* the Sanhedrin.

— ἄξων, *for the purpose of bringing.*

— ἐκεῖσε. Here put for ἐκεῖ. See xxi. 3.

9. The companions of St. Paul saw the light, but no distinct person; they heard the voice, but no distinct words. See ix. 7.

10. ὧν, by attraction for ἅ.

— τέτακται, *it hath been appointed.*

11. οὐκ ἐνέβλεπον, *I could not see.* ἐμβλέπω means, strictly, *I look at or on something.*

12. μαρτυρούμενος, *testified of,* *i.e.* well spoken of. Compare vi. 3 and xxvi. 22.

— τῶν κατοικούντων, *who were residing there,* in Damascus.

13. ἀνάβλεψον, *receive thy sight.* ἀναβλέπω means (1) I look up, (2) I recover my sight (Herod. ii. 3). Some take ἀνέβλεψα in *both* senses, *I recovered my sight and looked.*

14. προεχειρίσατο, *destined.* From προχειρίζομαι, *I make ready for use.* See xxvi. 16.

— τὸν δίκαιον, *the Just One.* See vii. 52.

15. αὐτῷ, *for Him.* Dative of *ministration.*

— ὧν = τούτων ἅ, *of those things which.* Compare Xen. Anab. i. 9, 25.

16. βάπτισαι, *submit to baptism.* The middle is used (where we might expect the passive) to denote that an action takes place *with the permission of the subject.*

17. προσευχομένου μου, *while I was praying.* The genitive used absolutely to express *the time* when something occurred. Here it follows the *dative,* as in Xen. An. i. 4. 12.

The genitive absolute is regularly used only when a new subject is introduced into the sentence, and not when the participle can be joined with any noun already belonging to the construction. Yet this rule is sometimes violated, in order to give greater prominence to a particular clause, as in Thuc. i. 114.

— ἐκστάσει, *a trance.* See note on x. 10.

19. ἤμην φυλακίζων. For this form of expression see note on xxi. 29.

20. ἐξεχεῖτο, *was being shed.* Imperf. pass. ἐκχέω.

— μάρτυρος. The word probably means *witness* here. The first place in which it is clearly used for one *who sealed his testimony with his blood* is Rev. xvii. 6. In the third century those who died for the faith were called *Martyrs;* those who suffered any persecution short of death *Confessors.*

22. λόγου. The word which excited their anger was *Gentiles* (ἔθνη).

— οὐ καθῆκον. With the ellipsis of ἐστί, *it is not fitting,* καθῆκον being participle of καθήκω: but the true reading is καθῆκεν, the imperfect, and the sense is, *he should not have been permitted to live,* referring to their attempt to kill him (xxi. 31).

23. ῥιπτούντων, *tossing about*, as a sign of excitement.

— ἀνετάζεσθαι αὐτὸν, *that he would have him examined.*

— ἐπιγνῷ, *might obtain full knowledge.*

25. προέτεινεν αὐτόν, *he was stretching him forward.* A better reading is προέτειναν, *they had stretched him forward*, the *aorist* being put for the *pluperfect.* The singular would refer to the centurion, the plural to the soldiers.

— τοῖς ἱμᾶσιν, *with the thongs*, i.e. the thongs with which the prisoner was lashed to a post in front of him, probably sloping away from the place where his feet were fastened, so that the body was stretched *forward.* Others explain it *for the thongs*, i.e. in preparation for the thongs of the whip.

— Ῥωμαῖον. For the law forbidding such an act, see xvi. 37; and compare Cic. Verr. ii. 5, 62 and 63.

28. κεφάλαιον is used for *a sum of money* in classical authors, but only when *capital* as opposed to *interest* is meant.

— ἐγὼ δὲ καὶ γεγέννημαι (πολίτης), *but I was also born a (citizen).* The *perfect* implies *I still am a citizen.* How St. Paul acquired the citizenship of Rome is not clear. He did not possess it as being a native of Tarsus (a free city, but not a *colonia* or *municipium*). Probably one of his ancestors acquired the freedom of Rome.

29. ἦν δεδεκώς. Compare xxi. 29.

30. τὸ τί. For the article attached to the *sentence* to call particular attention to it, see iv. 21.

8

CHAPTER XXIII.

1. πάσῃ συνειδήσει ἀγαθῇ, *with every good conscience*, i.e. with a consciousness of rectitude on every occasion. Compare xx. 19, and observe the meaning of πᾶς without the article.

— πεπολίτευμαι τῷ Θεῷ, *I have been loyal to God.* πολιτεύομαι means *I live as a citizen*, hence it means *I do my duty as a citizen*: it always implies *public* life, διαιτάομαι being used for *private* life, as in Thuc. vii. 77.

Observe the double dative: συνειδήσει is the dative of *manner*, Θεῷ is the dative of *ministration*.

2. Ananias was made High-priest in 48 A.D.; he was sent to Rome in 52 A.D. to answer before Claudius a charge of oppression brought by the Samaritans. He appears not to have lost his office on that occasion, but soon after the events recorded in this chapter he was deposed by Felix.

— τοῖς παρεστῶσιν, *those who stood by*, meaning *the servants* who were in waiting upon the Sanhedrin. Compare Luke xix. 24, and for a similar classical usage, Hom. Od. viii. 218.

3. τύπτειν σε μέλλει. A prophecy: Ananias was stabbed by the Sicarii during the last Jewish war.

— τοῖχε κεκονιαμένε, *thou whited wall.* Apparently a proverbial expression for a hypocrite, either from the use of plaster or stucco to *conceal the defects* of a wall, or from the custom prevalent among the Jews of *whitening sepulchres*, to warn passers-by of defilement. Compare Matt. xxiii. 27.

κονιάω means *I plaster with lime*, from κονία, which, in addition to its common meaning *dust*, is also used for any *fine powder*, and so for *lime powder*.

τοῖχος, *the wall of a house*; τεῖχος, *the wall of a city*.

3. καὶ παρανομῶν, *and yet transgressing the law*.

5. οὐκ ᾔδειν. These words are variously interpreted; thus—

(1) I did not know, from a defect of eye-sight.

(2) I did not remember, from a lapse of memory.

(3) I did not know, because he thought Ananias had been deposed from the office.

It is worth observing that the person presiding over the Sanhedrin was not on all occasions the High-priest. The President of the Sanhedrin was chosen for eminence in virtue and wisdom: often the High-priest was elected, but not always. Therefore it is possible that St. Paul did not know that the President on this occasion was the High-priest.

— ἄρχοντα, κ. τ. λ. The quotation is from Exod. xxii. 28.

6. υἱὸς Φαρισαίου. The best MSS. have Φαρισαίων, which would mean that his father, grandfather, and perhaps more remote ancestors, were Pharisees.

— κρίνομαι, *am placed on my trial*.

7. Pharisees. So called from an Aramaic word Perishin, *separated*.

Among their fundamental principles were the following :—

(1) That along with the written law there was a body of traditions, an oral law, equally binding on faithful Jews.

(2) That the Soul is imperishable, and that there will be a Resurrection of the Dead.

They are represented in the Gospels as hypocritical, covetous, self-righteous, and austere.

7. Sadducees.   Are said to have derived their name from a learned Scribe, Zadok, who lived about B.C. 280. It has been lately suggested that they may have been descendants of Zadok, the famous High-priest in the days of Solomon, and that they formed a kind of sacerdotal aristocracy, the High-priests belonging to their party, which certainly finds support from Acts v. 17. They held—

(1) That the written law alone was binding, and that oral traditions were worthless.

(2) That there will be no Resurrection of the Dead.

8. τὰ ἀμφότερα, *both of them.*   *Three* things are mentioned, but they are reducible to *two*, (1) the Resurrection, (2) the existence of Spiritual beings (ἄγγελος καὶ πνεῦμα).

The readings vary: if we have μηδὲ . . . μήτε, the two last things are *represented* under one head ; if μήτε . . . μήτε, they are specified as distinct, but must be *regarded* as coming under the same head.

9. Scribes.   A body of men who from very early times employed themselves in *copying* the Law with scrupulous minuteness, and who from the time of Ezra, himself a Scribe, became more and more prominent as

expounders of the Law, when Hebrew ceased to be the spoken language of the people. In our Lord's time they upheld the importance of the traditions, and corrupted the spirit of the law. They were far above the Priests in the estimation of their countrymen, and the Priest who did not become a Scribe remained in obscurity. They were ambitious, worldly-minded, and hypocritical.

9. διεμάχοντο, *stoutly protested*, or, *exerted themselves* (in his behalf).

— μὴ θεομαχῶμεν. These words are omitted in the best MSS.; something of the kind is *implied*, but the sentence is designedly left incomplete; the Pharisees spoke of the matter as doubtful and requiring caution.

10. στάσεως, *violent disputation*. The word στάσις is used for *faction, discord;* hence in later Greek it was used for *strife accompanied by violent language*. See xix. 40.

— εὐλαβηθείς *fearing*. The deponent εὐλαβέομαι means (1) *I act with caution* (Heb. xi. 7), (2) *I fear*. The latter meaning seems better in this passage.

— διασπασθῇ. Literally, *should be pulled asunder*.

— τὸ στράτευμα, *his troops*. Possessive force of the article.

11. διεμαρτύρω, *thou didst solemnly testify*. 2 pers. sing. 1 aor. διαμαρτύρομαι. See viii. 25.

— εἰς Ἰερουσαλήμ, *to Jerusalem*, the preaching being addressed to the city; so εἰς Ῥώμην, *to Rome*. Compare Mark i. 39; xiv. 9. Some explain this use of εἰς, where

we might expect ἐν, by supplying *when you have come.*
Compare viii. 40, and Thuc. vi. 16, end.

12. συστροφήν, *a plot,* called in verse 13 συνωμοσίαν,
a conspiracy. The word is used in xix. 40 for the *confusion* of a noisy crowd.

— ἀνεθεμάτισαν, *bound by a curse.* See verse 14.

— ἕως οὗ ἀποκτείνωσι, *till they should kill.* The
omission of ἄν is contrary to the usage of Greek *prose.*
The poets occasionally omit the particle, as Soph. Aj.
555. Compare Gal. iii. 19.

14. ἀναθέματι, κ.τ.λ., *we bound* (aorist) *ourselves by a
curse.* In classical Greek ἀνάθημα (from ἀνατίθημι, *I set
up* as a votive gift) is used for offerings presented to the
Gods, and so was used of that which was *devoted* to a
God; in this sense it occurs once in the New Testament,
of the gifts made to the Temple (Luke xxi. 5.) The form
ἀνάθεμα is peculiar to late Greek, and also means *that
which is devoted,* but in a *bad* sense, as of that which is
" accursed to the Lord " (Josh. vi. 17), *an accursed thing,*
or, as here, *the curse* invoked upon themselves by the
conspirators in the event of swerving from their purpose.

15. ἐμφανίσατε, *give information.* From ἐμφανίζω, *I
make clear.*

— σὺν τῷ συνεδρίῳ, *in conjunction with the Sanhedrin,*
i.e. not *you alone* (ὑμεῖς) but with the sanction and
authority of the Sanhedrin.

— διαγινώσκειν, *to investigate* (*thoroughly*). Lat. *cog-
noscere.* Compare xxv. 13.

15. τοῦ ἀνελεῖν, *for the purpose of slaying.* Genitive of *design.*

16. τὸ ἔνεδρον, *the lying in wait.* In classical Greek we should have τὴν ἐνέδραν.

19. κατ' ἰδίαν (χώραν), *to a private (place).*

20. συνέθεντο, *made* (aorist) *a conspiracy.*

— τοῦ ἐρωτῆσαι, *for the purpose of asking.* Genitive of *design.*

— μέλλων. This would refer to the Tribune. Some read μέλλον, referring to the Sanhedrin: others μέλλοντες, referring to the conspirators.

21. μὴ πεισθῇς, *be not persuaded.*

— τὴν ἐπαγγελίαν, *the promise.*

22. ἐνεφάνισας, *thou didst disclose.* Observe the change to the *direct* narration, and compare i. 4; xvii. 3.

23. τίνας δύο. We have, in English, no equivalent for this use of τίς. Compare Luke vii. 19; Acts xix. 14; and Thuc. viii. 100.

— στρατιώτας, *soldiers* of the legion; *legionaries; milites gravis armaturæ.*

— δεξιολάβους. A word of very late Greek, used of a peculiar description of *light-armed infantry.* It may be rendered *spearmen,* the deriv. being δεξιᾷ λαβεῖν, *to grasp with the right hand.* Another reading is δεξιοβόλους =*jaculantes dextra.*

— ἀπὸ τρίτης ὥρας, *from the third hour, i.e. at and after* the third hour. Compare Thuc. vii. 43, ἀπὸ πρώτου ὕπνου, and Hor. Ep. i. 14. 34, *mediâ de luce;* ἀπό and *de* having in those passages the meaning *immediately after.*

24. κτήνη. In classical Greek, *cattle.* Here used for *beasts of burden; sarcinaria jumenta* (Cæs. B. C. i. 81).

— παραστῆσαι, *that they should provide.* 1 aor. infinitive, not depending on any word expressed or understood, but used by way of *change from the direct to the indirect narration.* παραστῆναι occurs in the same irregularity of construction in Thuc. vi. 34.

— διασώσωσι, *might convey him safely all the way.*

— Felix was made Procurator of Judæa by Claudius, whose freedman he was, in A.D. 53. He ruled the province in a mean and cruel manner. His period of office was marked by seditious outbreaks, which he settled with vigour and punished the authors with severity. He was superseded by Festus about A.D. 60. He married Drusilla, daughter of Herod Agrippa I.

25. τύπον, which generally means in the New Testament *a pattern,* is here put for *a form of words,* like the Latin *exemplum* used for *the purport of a* letter.

26. χαίρειν, *sends greeting,* the epistolary infinitive. See xv. 23.

27. συλληφθέντα, *when he was apprehended.*

— ἐπιστάς, *coming suddenly upon* (them).

— αὐτόν. This pronoun is unnecessary, but it is inserted for the sake of *clearness,* since so many words come between τοῦτον and ἐξειλόμην.

27. σὺν τῷ στρατεύματι, *with my soldiers.* Possessive force of the article.

— μαθὼν ὅτι ῾Ρωμαῖός ἐστι. This was untrue.

28. ἐνεκάλουν, *they were accusing.* Imperfect ἐγκαλέω. See xix. 38.

30. μηνυθείσης, κ. τ. λ., *and a plot having been disclosed to me as being about to be made*, &c. For μέλλειν we should expect μελλούσης, the sentence being concluded with a different construction from that with which it commenced.

31. Antipatris, built by Herod the Great, and named in honour of his father Antipater, was about forty miles from Jerusalem, and twenty-six miles from Cæsarea.

32. "And on the following day they returned to the barracks, having left the horsemen to go with him; who, when they had entered," &c. Care is needed, in the arrangement of the English, to show that οἵτινες refers to ἱππεῖς.

35. διακούσομαι, *I will hear completely.*

— Πραιτωρίῳ, *the prætorium* or residence of the Roman Governor, built by Herod. The Latin word Prætorium was originally used for *the general's tent* in a camp. In later Greek πραιτώριον was used—

(1) For the residence of a Roman Governor.

(2) For a large room in the Governor's residence (Mark xv. 16).

CHAPTER XXIV.

1. μετὰ δὲ πέντε ἡμέρας, *after five days,* i.e. on the fifth day after the departure of St. Paul *for* Cæsarea, not *from* Cæsarea.

— πρεσβυτέρων τινῶν. A deputation from the Sanhedrin, not the whole body of the Elders.

2. ῥήτορος, *orator ;* one of the class of forensic pleaders, called by the Romans *causidici,* who found much employment in the provincial courts, especially when the proceedings, as in this case, were conducted in the Latin tongue.

— Τερτύλλου. A common Roman name, a diminutive from Tertius.

— ἐνεφάνισαν, *laid information.* 1 aor. ἐμφανίζω.

3. πολλῆς εἰρήνης, *profound peace.*

— διορθωμάτων, *acts of reformation.* Some read κατορθωμάτων, *happy results.*

— γινομένων, *being brought about.*

— προνοίας, *forethought* (Lat. *providentiœ*), a word applied in late Greek especially to the *providence* of the Gods.

— ἀποδεχόμεθα, *we acknowledge (it).* ἀποδέχομαι is used for *the willing acceptance of an opinion,* or, *the willing recognition of a favour.*

4. ἐπὶ πλεῖον, *longer (than is necessary), too long.*

— ἐνκόπτω, *detain.* This word of later Greek derives

its meaning from the practice of *cutting a trench* or *breaking up a road* in the way of an advancing army. It is the opposite of προκόπτω, which, from its original meaning of *cutting away* impediments, as trees, is used for *facilitating progress*.

4. ἀκοῦσαι συντόμως, *to give a brief hearing*.

— ἐπιεικείᾳ, from ἐπιεικής, *one who does not press his strict claims*, is here used for *gentleness* or *clemency*, as in Thuc. iii. 40. Observe also that ἐπιείκεια denotes *a habit*, and so here involves a compliment, *your usual gentleness*.

5. εὑρόντες γάρ. Here is an instance of *anakoluthon* (see xv. 23), for had the structure of the sentence thus commenced been carried out, we should have had in verse 6, ἐκρατήσαμεν αὐτόν, whereas the writer annexes this principal verb to the relative clause, ὅς . . . ἐπείρασε.

— λοιμόν, *pest*, i.e. *pestilent fellow*. λοιμός means (1) *a pestilence*, (2) as used of persons, *a plague, a pest*. *Pestis* is used in Latin just in the same way.

— πρωτοστάτην. Properly *one who stands first*, a military word, used (1) of the first man on the right of a line, (2) of each man in the front rank; hence *a leader*, *a ringleader*, as here.

— αἱρέσεως, *party, sect*. See note on v. 17.

8. παρ᾽ οὗ. It is doubtful whether these words refer to *Paul* or to *Lysias*. The question is complicated by the difficulties connected with the text, for the chief MSS. omit the whole sentence from καὶ κατὰ in 6, to ἐπὶ

σέ in 8, and in that case Paul must be the person from whom enquiry was to be made.

8. ἀνακρίνας, *having made an investigation.* See xii. 19.

— ἐπιγνῶναι, *to obtain full knowledge.*

9. συνέθεντο, *agreed, assented ;* but the true reading is συνεπέθεντο, *joined in the attack* on Paul. See Thuc. vi. 56.

— φάσκοντες, *asserting, affirming.*

10. ἐκ πολλῶν ἐτῶν, *for many years.* ἐκ indicates the commencement of the period *through which* something continues to exist, and so is stronger than ἀπό, which indicates the point of time *from which* something commenced. Comp. ix. 33, and xv. 21, with xv. 7.

— εὐθυμότερον, *the more cheerfully,* as having a competent judge, Felix having been six years in his office.

11. πλείους. Attic contraction of πλείονες.

— εἰσί μοι, *have passed over me.* The dative stands in statements of the time that has elapsed since a person performed a certain action. See Hom. Il. xxi. 155. Compare also Thuc. iii. 29.

— ἢ δεκαδύο. The chief MSS. omit ἢ in accordance with the Attic usage that, when a number follows πλείων, ἤ may be omitted without influencing the case of the number (Plat. Ap. 17, D). See also Ter. Ad. ii. 1. 46. If ἤ be omitted, δεκαδύο (Att. δώδεκα) might be regarded as the genitive. Compare Thuc. iv. 44, and Acts xxiii. 13.

11. ἀφ' ἧς = ἀπὸ τῆς ἡμέρας ᾗ, *from the day on which.* Compare Acts i. 2.

12. ἐπισύστασιν, *uproar, a riotous meeting.* A word of late Greek. Some read ἐπίστασιν, a classical word, with which the meaning is *exciting the attention*, or, *exciting a sudden attack.*

— κατὰ τὴν πόλιν, *about the city.*

13. παραστῆσαι means (1) *to present*, (2) *to prove*, as here. If με be added, a reading not confirmed by the chief MSS., we must understand παραστῆσαί με to mean *to prove me guilty.*

14. αἵρεσιν, *a sect;* referring to the word αἱρέσεως used by Tertullus. It is desirable not to render the word by *heresy* here, because the word αἵρεσις was not used in that sense, for the open espousal of a *fundamental* error, till the second century.

— οὕτω is here connected with the clause *that follows*, πιστεύων πᾶσι, κ. τ. λ., the meaning being *I serve . . . thus, namely, by believing, &c.*

— τῷ πατρῴῳ θεῷ. The phrase πατρῷοι θεοί was used for the tutelary gods of a family or people ; and as the Roman law allowed all men to worship the gods of their own nation, it seems probable that St. Paul is here asserting that from a Roman Governor's point of view he could not be deemed guilty of irreligion. See Thuc. ii. 71.

15. οὗτοι, *these men*, pointing to the Elders then present.

16. ἐν τούτῳ, *in conformity with this* belief. Compare Joh. xvi. 30.

— ἀσκῶ, *I exercise myself, I keep myself in constant training*, a meaning which the word has in Plat. Rep. 389 c. Modern editors omit the comma after ἀσκῶ, in which case the word means *I take pains.*

— πρὸς τὸν Θεόν, *in reference to God*, i.e. in respect of my duty to God.

17. δέ, *again.* He proceeds to reply to *another head* of the accusation, the profanation of the Temple. See ver. 6.

— δι᾽ ἐτῶν πλειόνων, *after an interval of several years,* πλείονες being used like *plures* in Latin. For the genitive of time with διά, compare Gal. ii. 1, and see also Acts i. 4, where the meaning is *during.* The interval to which St. Paul refers was one of four years.

— ἐλεημοσύνας ποιήσων, κ. τ. λ., *to bestow alms on my nation, and* (*to make*) *offerings* (*for myself*). The rendering *to bring alms*, though expressing the meaning, is not strictly correct. ποιέω may however be used for φέρω, just as in Latin *facio* is sometimes put for *affero* (Cic. Fam. xiv. 7 ; Tac. Hist. ii. 70).

18. ἐν οἷς, *in which occupations.* The relative is put in the *neuter*, though the antecedents to which it refers are *feminine*, either because they are *inanimate things* (Xen. Cyr. i. 3, 2), or to put the matter in a *general* way, as in xxvi. 12.

The true reading seems to be ἐν αἷς, *in presenting which offerings.*

18. ἡγνισμένον, *sanctified* as a Nazarite.

— τινὲς δέ. Supply οὐχ οὗτοι μέν, and render the passage thus, (*it was not these men who found me*) *but some Jews*, &c. It is a reply to the assertion of Tertullus that *the elders found* the Apostle engaged in these seditious practices.

19. δεῖ παρεῖναι, *ought to be present.* The Revised Version has *ought to have been here*, following the reading ἔδει παρεῖναι.

20. εἰπάτωσαν. This form of the 3 per. pl. of the imperative is common in the New Testament, as in xxv. 5. The *older* Attic writers use the abbreviated form, which is the same as the genitive plural of the participle, thus εἰπάντων.

The 1 aor. εἶπα is found in Attic : and this particular word εἰπάτωσαν is found in *later* Attic.

21. φωνῆς ἧς ἐκέκραξα, *cry, which I shouted out.* ἧς for ἥν by attraction. ἐκέκραξα is a reduplicated aorist.

22. ἀνεβάλετο αὐτούς, *deferred them*, *i.e.* adjourned the hearing of the case. Lat. *ampliavit eos*, there being here an allusion to the regular course taken by a judex in a matter requiring further consideration, which was to adjourn the case ; this was called *ampliatio*.

— ἀκριβέστερον εἰδώς, *because he knew more accurately*, *i.e.* than the opponents of St. Paul expected.

— τὰ περὶ τῆς ὁδοῦ, *the matters relating to the religion.* See ix. 2.

— διαγνώσομαι, *I will give you a decision.* An Athenian law-term.

22. τὰ καθ' ὑμᾶς, *on the matters relating to you.*

23. τηρεῖσθαι, *kept in custody.*

— ἄνεσιν, *indulgence;* his confinement was not to be too rigorous. Some explain the word to mean *personal liberty*, that he was not to be chained. See note on verse 27.

— κωλύειν, *that (the Centurion) should hinder.* Note the change of subject.

24. Drusilla was daughter of Herod Agrippa I., and sister of Herod Agrippa II. Felix persuaded her to leave her husband, Azizus, king of Emesa, and to become his wife, contrary to the Jewish law. Josephus tells us that she was the most beautiful woman of her time, and that she married Felix to escape ill-treatment from her sister Bernice, who was jealous of her.

— τῇ ἰδίᾳ γυναικί, *his own wife.*

— οὔσῃ 'Ιουδαίᾳ, *who was a Jewess*, simply to inform the reader of the fact ; or implying the desire of Drusilla to hear Paul, *because she was a Jewess.*

— εἰς Χριστόν, *on Christ,* or, *with respect to Christ,* who is the *object* of faith.

25. ἔμφοβος. Felix was a reckless reprobate. Tacitus says of him, "he thought he could perpetrate every sort of wickedness with impunity"; and "indulging in every kind of barbarity and lust, he exercised the power of a king in the spirit of a slave ".

— τὸ νῦν ἔχον, *for the present.* A phrase of late Greek.

25. καιρὸν μεταλαβών, *having obtained a convenient season*.

26. χρήματα. Felix knew that Paul was the bearer of money to Jerusalem, and he might suppose that the Christians would furnish funds to procure the release of their leader.

27. διετίας πληρωθείσης, *when two years were completed*, *i.e.* in A.D. 60.

— ἔλαβε διάδοχον, *received as a successor*.

— Festus was Procurator of Judæa for but a short time ; he probably died about two years after his appointment.

— χάριτας καταθέσθαι, *to lay up a stock of favours* (Herod. vi. 41 ; Thuc. i. 33), so that he might have friends in Judæa to support him in case an accusation should be made against him for misgovernment. The phrase is a metaphor taken from depositing money in a bank that it may be drawn out afterwards with interest.

— διδεμένον. The various kinds of imprisonment at this time are thus given by Conybeare and Howson (ii. 296) :

(1) *Custodia publica*, in the common prison.
(2) *Custodia libera*, when a man was committed to the charge of a magistrate or senator. Sall. Cat. 47.
(3) *Custodia militaris*, in which the prisoner was given in charge to a soldier, whose left hand was chained to the prisoner's right.
(4) *Observatio*, when the soldier was always with the prisoner, but was not chained to him.

CHAPTER XXV.

1. ἐπιβάς, *having reached.* Seldom with a *dative* (Thuc. 7, 70). See also xxvii. 2.

— ἐπαρχίᾳ, *province.* The word Provincia was applied not only to the districts governed by Prætors and Proconsuls, but also to the sub-divisions under the government of Procurators. Judæa was part of the Province of Syria; the governor of Judæa was called Procurator; the governor of Syria, Præses or Proconsul.

The Governor of Judæa was *nominally* subordinate to the Governor of Syria, but within his own province he was quite unfettered in his acts. See Tac. Hist. ii. 5.

2. ἐνεφάνισαν αὐτῷ, *laid an information before him.*

— ὁ ἀρχιερεύς. The High-priest at the time was Ishmael.

3. κατ᾽ αὐτοῦ, *against him, i.e.* against Paul.

— μεταπέμψηται, *he would send for.*

— ποιοῦντες, *they (at the same time) making.* The *present* participle is used to show that at the very time of making the request they were planning to kill Paul.

Observe the two participles, αἰτούμενοι and ποιοῦντες, *not connected by any conjunction,* standing in different relations to the verb παρεκάλουν, the former expressing *the manner* in which the request was made, the latter *the circumstances accompanying* the request; and compare Hom. Il. xi. 212.

5. οἱ δυνατοί, *they who have authority* to represent the nation.

— ἐν αὐτοῖς, *among them, i.e.* in Jerusalem. But the true reading is ἐν ὑμῖν.

7. περιέστησαν, *stood round (Paul).*

— πολλὰ καὶ βαρέα, *many weighty.* A common Greek idiom. Sometimes καί appears to be emphatic = *atque, et quidem,* and so it may be here *many, and what is more, weighty.*

— αἰτιώματα. A word of late Greek, for which classical authors use αἰτιάματα.

— ἀποδεῖξαι, *to prove* by corroborative testimony.

8. τὶ ἥμαρτον, *did I commit any single offence.*

9. χάριν καταθέσθαι, *to lay up a stock of favour.*

— ἐπ᾽ ἐμοῦ, *in my presence.* Festus proposed to be present at the trial of Paul before the Sanhedrin. For this use of ἐπί compare xxvi. 2.

10. Καίσαρος. Nero was Emperor at this time, A.D. 60.

— οὐδὲν ἠδίκησα, *I did no single act of wrong.*

— κάλλιον, *very well.* The comparative is sometimes used where the positive would be more natural.

11. ἀδικῶ, *I am guilty.* For this use of the present of this verb with a perfect signification compare Thuc. iii. 65.

— οὐ παραιτοῦμαι τὸ ἀποθανεῖν, *I do not seek to escape from death.* παραιτέομαι is most commonly used with an accusative of the person from whom something is *obtained by entreaty;* but it is also used in the sense *I avert by entreaty, I deprecate,* with an accusative of *the thing to be averted.*

11. εἰ . . . οὐδέν. "It is universally acknowledged that εἰ does not always preserve its hypothetical force, but may be put for ὅτι or ὡς to express a simple fact; or for ἐπεί, *since,* as a hypothetical consequence where, however, no *doubt* is implied; or for πότερον, *whether,* as an alternative." Cope on Arist. Rhet. App. C. So here the meaning is, *but the fact being that I have committed no offence.*

— οὐδέν, κ. τ. λ., *no one of the things of which* (ὧν = τούτων ἅ) *these men accuse me is true.*

— χαρίσασθαί με αὐτοῖς, *to make a gift of me to them,* i.e. to give me up simply to gratify them. Compare Aristoph. Eq. 54.

— Καίσαρα ἐπικαλοῦμαι. Appeal to the Emperor was the right of every Roman citizen.

12. τοῦ συμβουλίου, *his council, i.e.* persons resident in the province who assisted the Procurator in legal questions. Lat. *consiliarii* or *assessores.*

13. 'Αγρίππας.   Herod Agrippa II., son of Herod Agrippa I.   When his father died he was only seventeen years old, and the Emperor Claudius considered him too young to govern his father's kingdom.   But he subsequently received various districts, and had the title of King, the charge of the Temple at Jerusalem, and the appointment of the High-priest.   In the last Jewish war he took part with the Romans, and after the fall of Jerusalem he lived in retirement at Rome. He died A.D. 100, and was the last prince of the house of Herod.

13. Βερνίκη.   Bernice or Berenice was daughter of Herod Agrippa I., and sister of Herod Agrippa II. and Drusilla.   She married her uncle, Herod, king of Chalcis.   She next lived, as it was generally supposed, with her brother as his mistress.   She then married the king of Cilicia, then became mistress of Vespasian, and finally lived with his son Titus, who unwillingly sent her away from Rome because the Romans hated her.

— ἀσπασάμενοι, *having saluted*, must be explained as being equivalent to *and saluted*.   Compare xviii. 27.

14. ἀνέθετο, *laid before*, with a view to *consultation*, as in Gal. ii. 2.   The word has no such meaning in classical Greek, but it is derived from the meanings, *I refer, I entrust*, which ἀνατίθημι did sometimes bear.

15. δίκην, *sentence, condemnation* = καταδίκην, which the chief MSS. have.

16. ἔχοι. The *optative* is used because Festus is quoting in indirect narration the words which he addressed to the Jews. In speaking to them he would use the *subjunctive* ἔχῃ.

— τόπον, *occasion, opportunity*. A late meaning of the word.

17. ἀναβολήν, *delay* or *adjournment*. See note on xxiv. 22.

18. περὶ οὗ, *round whom*, as in verse 7.

— ἐπέφερον, *imputed* to him. The true reading is ἔφερον, altered to ἐπέφερον as the more usual expression, *e.g.* Herod. i. 26 ; Thuc. vi. 76.

— ὧν = ἐκείνων ἅ, *of the things which*.

19. δεισιδαιμονίας, *religious cautiousness* or *fear of God*. It seems unlikely that Festus should use the word in the sense, which it sometimes bears, of *superstition* when he was addressing a Jewish king. Compare xvii. 22.

20. τὴν περί, κ. τ. λ., *as to the manner of investigating this matter*. Some read εἰς τὴν . . . but without authority. Compare Thuc. v. 40, ἀποροῦντες ταῦτα.

— ἔλεγον εἰ βούλοιτο. The construction is very difficult. We must take it thus, *I asked whether he were willing*, or, *I proposed, if he were willing, that*. See also note on xvi. 22.

21. τοῦ Σεβαστοῦ, *the Emperor*. The word σεβαστός is the Greek rendering of *Augustus, Venerable*, the title

conferred by the Senate on Octavianus, and borne by all his successors on the Imperial throne.

21. διάγνωσιν, *judgment.* See xxiv. 22.

22. ἐβουλόμην, *I was wishing,* i.e. *I should like.*

23. φαντασίας, *pomp.* A late use of the word derived from the original meaning, *a displaying.* Lat. *ostentatio.*

23. τὸ ἀκροατήριον, *the audience-chamber.*

— χιλιάρχοις, *tribunes,* commanding the Roman Cohorts, of which Josephus mentions *five* as being stationed at Cæsarea.

26. ἀσφαλές τι, *anything accurate.*

— τῷ Κυρίῳ, *to our Sovereign Lord.* The Emperors after Tiberius allowed themselves to be styled Κύριος and *Dominus.*

— τῆς ἀνακρίσεως, *the investigation.*

— τι γράψω, *something about which I shall write.* γράψω is fut. indic. But the better reading is γράψαι, *to write about.*

27. ἄλογον, *absurd.* The opposite of εὔλογον, Thuc. vi. 76.

CHAPTER XXVI.

1. ἐκτείνας, *having stretched forth.* As one about to make a set speech, St. Paul prefaced his words with the usual *action* of the orator.

2. ἥγημαι, *1 have thought.* Perfect of ἡγέομαι.

3. μάλιστα γνώστην, *intimately acquainted.*

— ὄντα σε. The accusative depends upon a word easily supplied from ἥγημαι, as, for instance, ἐπιστά-μενος, which is the word actually used in the com-mencement of the Apostle's address to Felix (xxiv. 10). Compare Thuc. i. 36.

— κατὰ 'Ιουδαίους, *among the Jews, belonging to the Jews.* Compare xvii. 28.

4. μὲν οὖν, *now.* These particles are used in *transi-tions* in a narrative (xxvi. 9: viii. 4; xi. 19), and at the commencement of an *argument* after some prefatory remarks, as here.

— βίωσις, *manner of life; ratio vivendi.* A very rare word of late Greek. The word generally used for manner of life in the N. T. is ἀναστροφή, *e.g.* i. 13.

— ἀπ' ἀρχῆς, *from the very first.*

5. προγινώσκοντες, *being previously acquainted.*

5. ἄνωθεν, *from the very beginning*, i.e. *from my earliest years*.

— αἵρεσιν, *party*. See note on v. 17.

— θρησκείας, *religion*, with particular reference to *external forms*.

— ἔζησα. Not classical, for ζῶ has fut. βιώσομαι, perf. βεβίωκα, aor. ἐβίων.

6. ἐπ᾽ ἐλπίδι, *with respect to the hope*.

— κρινόμενος, *on my trial*.

7. εἰς ἣν (ἐπαγγελίαν), *to which promise*.

— ἐν ἐκτενείᾳ = ἐκτενῶς, *assiduously*. See xii. 5.

8. The indicative ἐγείρει seems to indicate that he is referring to the Resurrection of Christ as *a fact about which he had no doubt*. Compare verse 23 and xxv. 11.

10. τὴν ἐξουσίαν, *the authority* to do so.

— ἀναιρουμένων αὐτῶν, *when they were being put to death*.

— κατήνεγκα ψῆφον, *I gave a vote against them*. The natural meaning of these words is that St. Paul was a member of a judicial court, the Sanhedrin, by which the Christians were condemned. Since, however, there is no other mention made of the Apostle being a member of the Sanhedrin, some prefer to explain the expression differently ; as—

(1) I acquiesced in the sentence.

(2) I carried down (from Jerusalem to other places) the sentence.

The Sanhedrin had not the power of inflicting death after A.D. 30.

11. τιμωρῶν, *taking vengeance on.*

— ἠνάγκαζον, *I tried to compel them.* Observe the *imperfect.*

— βλασφημεῖν, *to blaspheme,* lit. *to revile (Jesus).* The word, deriv. from βλάπτω and φήμη, originally meant *to speak ill of.*

— ἕως καὶ εἰς, *as far as even to.*

— τὰς ἔξω πόλεις, *the foreign cities,* i.e. beyond Palestine.

12. ἐν οἷς, *in which occupations.* Compare xxiv. 18.

13. ἡμέρας μέσης, *at mid-day.* The moment of time in which an action takes place is expressed by the *genitive.*

— πρὸς κέντρα λακτίζειν, *to kick against the goad,* a proverb, taken from the stupidity of an ox that, by kicking back against the goad, makes the point penetrate deeper.

16. ὤφθην σοι, *I appeared to thee.*

— προχειρίζομαι, means (1) *I take into my hand;* (2) *I make ready for myself;* (3) *I choose,* as here.

16. ὧν εἶδες = τούτων ἃ εἶδες, *of the things which you saw.*

— ὧν ὀφθήσομαι = τούτων ἃ (or, οἷς) ὀφθήσομαι, *of the things in which I will appear to thee,* where ἃ may be taken = δι᾽ ἅ. Comp. Soph. O. T., 788, and Thuc. ii. 63.

17. ἐξαιρούμενος, *delivering.* Some take it to mean *selecting,* but it is hard to see how St. Paul could be said to be chosen *from the Gentiles.*

18. τοῦ ἐπιστρέψαι, *that they may turn.* Genitive of *tendency* or *result.* See note on xv. 20.

— τοῦ λαβεῖν, *that they may receive.* Genitive of the final *result.*

— κλῆρον, *a portion.* See note on i. 17. The word κλῆρος and its derivatives, κληρονόμος, κληρονομία, and κληρονομέω, are frequently used with reference to the *spiritual inheritance* of the Saints. As Palestine was divided by lot among the tribes (Numb. xxvi. 55; Acts xiii. 19), it was natural for a Jew to speak of a similar distribution of the Messiah's kingdom among the Saints (Matt. v. 5; Col. i. 12).

— πίστει, *by faith.* *Instrumental* dative.

20. Ἱεροσολύμοις, *at Jerusalem.* *Local* dative.

— εἰς, *unto.* The preaching is said to be addressed *to the district,* as in xxiii. 11. The chief MSS. omit εἰς, and the accusative then denotes the space over which the preaching extended.

20. ἀπήγγελλον, *I was preaching.* Some read incorrectly ἀπαγγέλλων.

21. διαχειρίσασθαι, *to slay*, only here and v. 30 in N. T.

22. οὖν, *so then.* οὖν points strongly to what has gone before, so as to connect the premisses and the conclusion as one thought. The meaning here is: taking into consideration the danger to which I was exposed, I come to the conclusion that I owe my safety to the assistance of God. Compare Thuc. vii. 29; and Dem. F. L. 58.

— ἕστηκα, *I stand, I maintain my position.* So *steti* is used in Liv. v. 44.

— μαρτυρόμενος, κ. τ. λ., *testifying to small and great.* But some read—

— μαρτυρούμενος, κ. τ. λ. *testified of by small and great.*

— ὧν = τούτων ἅ.

23. εἰ, *if.* He puts it as a supposition *about which he has no doubt*, since the indicative μέλλει follows. See note on xxv. 11. To understand this verse we must compare it with xvii. 3. It is there said that St. Paul proved from the Scriptures that the Messiah had to suffer and to rise from the dead. Here he says his teaching was in accordance with the teaching of Moses and the Prophets, assuming that his hypothesis that the Messiah had to suffer and to rise from the dead was true. If that hypothesis were false, his deductions from Scripture were unfounded, and his teaching differed from that of Moses and the Prophets.

23. παθητός, *liable to suffering.* Lat. *patibilis.*

— πρῶτος ἐξ ἀναστάσεως νεκρῶν, *he first by a resurrection from the dead.*

24. τὰ πολλὰ γράμματα, *thy multifarious learning.*

25. σωφροσύνη, *sobermindedness* is the opposite of μανία.

26. οὐδέν, *in any way.*

— τοῦτο, *this,* involving all the circumstances connected with the rise and spread of Christianity: all which had occurred, not in a secret manner (ἐν γωνίᾳ), but in and about the chief cities of Palestine and Syria.

28. ἐν ὀλίγῳ, *with little trouble.* The objections to the rendering *almost* are—

(1) That *almost* would be expressed by ὀλίγου (Thuc. iv. 124) or παρ᾽ ὀλίγον.

(2) That it compels us to give a meaning to ἐν μεγάλῳ in the next verse which the phrase cannot well bear.

28. πείθεις. Another reading is πείθῃ, *you are persuaded.*

— γενέσθαι, *that I have become.* Agrippa probably spoke sarcastically, implying that his conversion would require much greater trouble than Paul had yet bestowed upon it.

For γενέσθαι, editors now usually read ποιῆσαι, and

render με πείθεις Χριστιανὸν ποιῆσαι, *thou wouldst fain make me a Christian.*

29. εὐξαίμην ἄν, *I would pray;* if I were allowed to express my desire.

— ἐν μεγάλῳ, *with much labour.* Some read ἐν πόλλῳ, with the same meaning.

31. πράσσει, *does.* The present is used because they are speaking of the *general tenor* of the Apostle's proceedings.

CHAPTER XXVII.

1. ἐκρίθη. Used impersonally, *it was determined.*

— τοῦ ἀποπλεῖν ἡμᾶς, *that we should sail away.* Genitive of *design.*

— ἑτέρους may mean *of another class,* not *Christian* prisoners, for ἕτερος implies a difference of *kind,* which is not involved in ἄλλος. See Lightfoot on Gal., i. 6, 7. But it may be used as in Thuc. viii. 102, ἑτέρας, where one might expect ἄλλας.

— σπείρης σεβαστῆς may be rendered *of the Augustan Cohort,* or, *of the Imperial Cohort.* We know that *Augusta* was a title given to several of the Roman Legions.

2. Ἀδραμυττήνῳ, *belonging to Adramyttium,* on the coast of Mysia.

2. μέλλοντι πλεῖν, *on the point of sailing.* μέλλοντες is a reading of no authority; with it we must render *since we were intending to sail.*

— τοὺς κατὰ τὴν 'Ασίαν τόπους, *to the places along the coast of Asia.* Accusative of *direction;* a classical construction. See Eur. Hel. 1590.

— 'Αριστάρχου. Who was with St. Paul at Ephesus (xix. 29), and who seems to have remained with the Apostle during his imprisonment at Rome (Col. iv. 10 ; Philem. 24).

3. κατήχθημεν, *we put into land.* See note on xviii. 21.

— Σιδῶνα. Sidon or Zidon was an important city, about twenty miles north of Tyre, lying in a fertile plain between the Lebanon and the sea. It had a fine harbour.

— ἐπέτρεψε (αὐτῷ) πορευθέντα. Lit. *gave (him) permission, that having gone.* For the accusative, following the dative, see xv. 22.

3. ἐπιμελείας τυχεῖν, *to obtain attention,* probably by receiving from his friends such things as might be of service to him in his voyage.

4. ὑπεπλεύσαμεν, *we sailed under the lee* of Cyprus. They put Cyprus between them and the wind, and passed on the *north* of the island.

5. διαπλεύσαντες, *having sailed across.*

6. πλέον, *on her voyage, bound* for Italy. The ship was laden with corn. Great stores of grain were regularly sent from *Egypt* to Rome. This ship may have been driven to Myra by the westerly wind; but in any case a ship going from Alexandria to Rome would stand to the north, so as to make the land of Asia Minor.

— ἐνεβίβασεν, *embarked.* 1 aor. ἐμβιβάζω, *I put on board.*

7. μόλις, *with difficulty.* The wind was probably *north-west*, under which the ship might work up slowly from Myra to Cnidus, the promontory of Caria, now *Cape Crio*, which projects between the islands of Cos and Rhodes.

— μὴ προσεῶντος, κ. τ. λ., *since the wind did not allow us to go in the direct course*, which would have been *north* of Crete. The modern name of Crete is *Candia*.

— ὑπεπλεύσαμεν, *we sailed under the lee*, keeping along the *eastern* shore of Crete and passing round Salmone, the extreme eastern point of the island, so as to get to the *southern* shore.

8. παραλεγόμενοι αὐτήν, *coasting along it, i.e.* working up along the southern coast of Crete, till they reached the Fair Havens, a harbour about midway in the southern coast, somewhat east of *Cape Matala.*

9. τοῦ πλοός, *the voyage.* The usual form is πλοῦς, πλοῦ; but in late Greek they made it πλοῦς, πλοός.

9. τὴν νηστείαν, *the Fast*, the day of Atonement, kept on the 10th of Tisri, which would be early in October. The ancients generally regarded the sea as closed from November to March.

10. θεωρῶ ὅτι . . . μέλλειν. A mixture of two constructions, θεωρῶ ὅτι μέλλει, and θεωρῶ μέλλειν, from hasty writing.

— ὕβρεως, *violence*, i.e. hard usage from the storm.

11. τῷ ναυκλήρῳ. Either *the owner of the ship*, or more probably *the captain of the ship*, as in Æsch. Supp. 174.

12. ἀνευθέτου, *inconveniently situated*.

— ἔθεντο βουλήν, *advised*.

— κἀκεῖθεν = καὶ ἐκεῖθεν, *from that place also*.

— Φοίνικα. Accus. of Φοῖνιξ, *Phœnix*, which is identified with the modern *Lutro*.
" This harbour faces the east, but having an island in front which shelters it ; it has two entrances, one looking to the north-east, and the other to the south-east." —Smith's *Voyage of St. Paul*.

— βλέποντα κατὰ λίβα καὶ κατὰ χῶρον. The natural interpretation of these words would be, *looking towards the south-west and north-west;* but since such an aspect is *precisely the contrary* of the bearings of *Lutro*, it has been suggested that κατά may here mean *in the direction of*, i.e. in the direction *towards which*, and not to the point of the compass *from which*, the winds blow. This is in

10

a slight degree confirmed by the use of κατά instead of πρός or εἰς, which would seem the natural words to use with βλέπω in the sense of looking *towards*, as in Xen. Mem. iii. 8, 9; Soph. Aj. 514.   Again, κατά in composition with words denoting geographical position is exactly opposite in meaning to πρός: thus κατάβορρος means *sheltered from the north*, whereas πρόσβορρος means *facing the north*.   Observe also that κατά often means *in a line with*.   See especially Thuc. vi. 104 and vi. 97.

12. λίβα.   Accus. of λίψ, the Greek name for the south-west wind, called by the Romans *Africus*.   The word is connected with Λιβύη, *Africa*, or, as some think, with λείβω, *I pour forth*, because it brought *rain*.

— χῶρον.   Accus. of χῶρος, the Greek form of Corus or Caurus, the north-west wind.

13. ὑποπνεύσαντος, *having sprung up gently*.

— κεκρατηκέναι, *that they had gained*, *i.e.* that their purpose was as good as accomplished.

— ἄραντες, *having loosed thence*.   Compare Thuc. vi. 104.

— ἆσσον, *nearer* than they could before.   Comparative of ἀγχοῦ.   Compare Seneca Agam. 107:

Remo terras propiore legit.

There is a reading Ἆσσον, as though a *place* in Crete were specified, *having weighed anchor for* (or *from*) *Assos*, but nothing can be made out of it.

14. ἔβαλε, *rushed*.   An *intransitive* use of βάλλω. Hom. Il. xi. 722.

14. κατ' αὐτῆς, *down from it, i.e.* from the island. Some take it to refer to the ship, *against it*, but the objection to this is that we should expect αὐτοῦ, to agree with τοῦ πλοίου.

— τυφωνικός, *violent.* From τυφώς, *a whirlwind, a furious storm.*

— 'Ευροκλύδων. It is generally admitted that this is a corruption of the true reading 'Ευρακύλων = Euraquilo, a north-easterly wind, strictly the wind from E.N.E.

15. συναρπασθέντος, *being snatched and carried off.* Compare Thuc. vi. 104.

— ἀντοφθαλμεῖν, *to face, to resist.*

— ἐπιδόντες, *having given up* ourselves, or, the ship.

16. ὑποδραμόντες, *running under the lee* of Clauda, now called *Gozzo*, a small island south-west of Cape *Matala*.

— περικρατεῖς. A late word, *conquering, possessed of.*

17. ἦν ἄραντες, *and having taken it on board.* Observe carefully that the *relative* in Greek and Latin often corresponds to the *demonstrative* pronoun, with such a conjunction as the case requires (*and, for,* &c.) in English.

— βοηθείαις, *supports.*

17. ὑποζωννύντες, *under-girding*, by passing ropes round the middle of the ship, to keep her planks from starting. For this operation (called by our seamen "frapping") ropes, called ὑποζώματα, were kept in the Athenian ships.

— τὴν σύρτιν, *the Syrtis*. The larger Syrtis, now the Gulf of *Sidra*, on the African coast; a bight much dreaded by the ancients from its shallow waters and uncertain currents.

— ἐκπέσωσι, *they should be wrecked*. A regular use of ἐκπίπτω.

— χαλάσαντες τὸ σκεῦος, *having lowered the gear*, is the rendering given in Smith's *Voyage of St. Paul*, where the rendering of the Authorized Version, *strake sail*, is censured as erroneous. The word σκεῦος is used for any *implement*, and in the plural it is put for the *rigging* of a ship as distinguished from the *sails* (Thuc. vii. 24). So that here τὸ σκεῦος is used in the singular with a *collective* force, for such masts and yards as happened at the time to be set, all of which were got down upon the deck.

18. χειμαζομένων, *being tossed by the storm*. Thuc. vi. 104.

— ἐκβολήν, *a casting out*, the word used, like *jactura*, for throwing out part of the cargo to lighten a ship in a storm.

19. τὴν σκευήν, *the equipment* or *the furniture* of the ship, meaning such things as were commonly used for cooking, sleeping, &c.

19. For ἐρρίψαμεν, *we cast*, the best MSS. have ἔρριψαν, *they cast*.

20. ἐπιφαινόντων, *showing light*, as in Luke i. 79.

— ἐπικειμένου, *pressing upon us*. The word used for *unremitting* attacks.

— περιῃρεῖτο, *was stripped away*. An emphatic word, implying stripping away on *every side*, as the leaves from a tree. Used again in verse 40. See Thuc. iii. 11.

21. ἀσιτίας, *abstinence from food*, partly from mental anxiety, and partly from loss of provisions damaged by the salt water.

— κερδῆσαί τε, *so as to have gained immunity from*. The verb κερδαίνω, of which κερδήσω is a *late* future (in Attic κερδανῶ), is used in late Greek in the sense, *I acquire immunity from, I avoid loss from*.

22. πλήν, *except (the loss)*. πλήν is here an adverb, and ἀποβολὴ ἔσται may be supplied, *but there shall be a loss of the ship*.

24. κεχάρισται, *hath bestowed as a favour*. χαρίζομαι is a word which implies *releasing from danger*, here and in iii. 14, or *consigning to danger* (xxv. 11) ; and in each case *as a favour to another*.

26. ἐκπεσεῖν, *be wrecked, be cast away*, as in verse 17.

27. διαφερομένων, *driven to and fro*.

27. Ἀδρίᾳ. Ancient geographers distinguish the *Sea* of Adria from the *Gulf* of Adria. The latter is that which is now called the Adriatic Sea or Gulf of Venice. The former, with which we are concerned in this passage, extended from Crete to Malta.

— ὑπενόουν, *surmised*. Probably from hearing the breakers.

— προσάγειν αὐτοῖς, *was approaching them*. St. Luke uses the language of seamen, to whom the land appears to approach.

28. βολίσαντες, *having sounded*. From βολίς, *the sounding lead*.

— ὀργυιά, *a fathom* = 6 feet. From ὀρέγω, *I stretch*, because the measure was strictly the length of the outstretched arms.

29. τραχεῖς τόπους, *rough places*, *i.e.* ledges of rocks.

— πρύμνης. Ancient ships generally anchored from the prow, but they had hawse-holes aft to enable the crew to anchor *by the stern*. The object of this in the present case was to keep the head of the ship towards the shore, so that when the anchors were cut she might be carried *stem on* to the beach.

30. προφάσει is here adverbial, *nominally, under a pretence* (Thuc. vi. 76 ; vii. 13).

— ὡς μελλόντων, *as though they were about*. The genitive absolute is often used with ὡς to express the *thought* or *pretext* under which something is spoken or done.

32. ἐκπεσεῖν, *fall and drift away.*

33. προσδοκῶντες, *waiting for deliverance.*

34. πρός with the genitive means sometimes *in favour of,* as here. Comp. Thuc. v. 105.

37. αἱ πᾶσαι, *in all* (xix. 7). ψυχαί, *persons,* as in ii. 41. The number of persons on board is given by some MSS. as 76, by others as 276.

38. κορεσθέντες, *having been satisfied.* 1 aor. pass. κορέννυμι.

— τὸν σῖτον, *the corn* with which the ship was laden ; part of which had been thrown over before. See verse 18.

39. κόλπον, *a creek ;* now called St. Paul's Bay.

— αἰγιαλόν, *a beach.* The proper word for a low, sandy beach, as distinguished from ἀκτή, a high and rocky shore.

— εἰς ὅν refers to αἰγιαλόν. See verse 40.

— ἐξῶσαι, *to strand.* 1 aor. inf. ἐξωθέω. Thuc. viii. 105. Some read ἐκσῶσαι, *to bring safe to shore.*

40. περιελόντες, *having cut away all round.* See note on verse 20.

— εἴων, *they let* (*them*) *go ;* they had no further use for the anchors.

— ἀνέντες, *having unlashed.* 2 aor. part. ἀνίημι.

40. τὰς ζευκτηρίας, *the bands* of the rudders. Ancient ships were steered by two paddles, one on each side of the stern, acting through a porthole.

— τὸν ἀρτέμονα, *the foresail*, a small sail at the prow.

— τῇ πνεούσῃ (αὔρᾳ), *to the blowing breeze.*

41. διθάλασσον, *where two seas met.* There is a small island in St. Paul's Bay, close to the shore; the sea rushing into the bay strikes the outer point of this island, which causes it to divide and *meet again* at the inner point.

— ἐπώκειλαν, *they ran aground.* 1 aor. ἐποκέλλω.

— ἐρείσασα, *being fixed.* 1 aor. ἐρείδω, which is sometimes transitive, *I set against*, sometimes intransitive, *I lean against.* The bottom of St. Paul's Bay is of mud, graduating into *tenacious clay.*

— ἐλύετο, *was being broken, was gradually going to pieces.*

— ὑπὸ τῆς βίας, by the violence (of the waves) τῶν κυμάτων being omitted in the chief MSS.

44. ἐπὶ σανίσιν . . . ἐπί τινων. The variation of the cases is probably accidental. Generally ἐπί with the local dative denotes *entire* superposition, with the local genitive, *partial* superposition.

CHAPTER XXVIII.

1. ἐπέγνωσαν, *they discovered* (some read ἐπέγνωμεν, *we discovered*), or it may be *knew for certain*, a common use of ἐπιγινώσκω.

— Μελίτη. The notion that this was not Malta, but a small island, now *Meleda*, in the Gulf of Venice, is rejected by the best commentators. It arose from a mistake as to the meaning of the word 'Αδρίᾳ in xxvii. 27.

2. βάρβαροι. So called as being neither Greeks nor Romans. The island was colonized by the Phœnicians.

— οὐ τὴν τυχοῦσαν, *of no ordinary description.* See xix. 11.

— τὸν ἐφεστῶτα, *that was then falling.*

3. ἔχιδνα, *a viper.* Venomous snakes are not found in Malta, but they may have disappeared when the woods were cleared away.

4. οὐκ εἴασεν, *did not permit.* Aorist of ἐάω.

6. πίμπρασθαι, *to become inflamed (and swollen).*

— αὐτῶν προσδοκώντων, *while they kept waiting.*

— ἄτοπον, *out of place,* and so *strange, unusual.*

— μεταβαλόμενοι, *having changed their minds,* as in Thuc. viii. 90.

7. ὑπῆρχε χωρία, *were estates.* Observe the *plural.* Thuc. i. 106. χωρίον (dim. of χῶρος or χώρα), a farm or *private* estate.

— τῷ πρώτῳ, *belonging to the chief man.* Dative of *especial reference,* as in iii. 6.

— Ποπλίῳ, *Publius.* Perhaps he held an official position, as an inscription has been found in which a man is called πρῶτος Μελιταίων.

8. συνεχόμενον, *distressed.* See note on xviii. 5, and Thuc. ii. 49.

10. τιμαῖς, *honours,* implying *gifts.* See 1 Tim. v. 17.

11. παρασήμῳ, a noun, *with the sign (of).* The word for figure-head in Thuc. vi. 31 is σημεῖον.

— Διοσκούροις, *the Dioscuri,* sons of Zeus, whose names were Castor and Pollux ; the guardian deities of sailors.

12. καταχθέντες, *having put into land.* See xviii. 21.

— Συρακούσας. Syracuse is situated on the eastern coast of Sicily, about eighty miles N.N.E. of Malta.

13. περιελθόντες, *having made a circuitous passage.* The meaning of this is not very clear: some take it to refer to the way in which the vessel tacked about with an unfavourable wind ; others prefer the supposition that the vessel hugged the winding shore of Sicily, instead of making a straight run to Rhegium.

13. περιελόντες is the reading of the chief MSS., apparently meaning *having cast loose*.

— 'Ρήγιον. Rhegium, on the coast of Italy, just at the southern entrance to the straits of Messina. It is now called *Reggio*.

— ἐπιγενομένου, *having afterwards set in.* Thuc. vi. 26.

— δευτεραῖοι, *on the second day of our voyage* from Rhegium. The Greeks employed adjectives in αἷος to express *the time when* anything happened; thus πεμπταῖοι ἀφίκοντο, *they arrived on the fifth day.* So in Joh. xi. 39, τεταρταῖός ἐστι, *he has been dead four days.*

— Ποτιόλους. Puteoli, now *Pozzuoli*, in the north eastern angle of the Bay of Naples. It was the principal port of Southern Italy. A road from Puteoli joined the Appian Way at Capua.

14. ἐπ᾿ αὐτοῖς is to be taken *after* ἐπιμεῖναι, *to remain with them.* Xen. Anab. 7, 2, 1.

15. εἰς ἀπάντησιν ἡμῖν, *for a meeting with us*, ἡμῖν being put in the *dative* because the person *met* is put in that case.

— 'Αππίου Φόρου. Appii Forum was a well-known station on the Appian Way, the great road which led from Rome to Capua, and then branched off to Brundisium. The name of the station was probably due to Appius Claudius, who first constructed the road. It was forty-three miles from Rome.

15. Τριῶν Ταβερνῶν, *Tres Tabernœ, Three Taverns,* a station on the Appian Way, thirty-three miles from Rome.

16. τῷ στρατοπεδάρχῃ, *the Prefect of the Prætorian Guard,* probably at this time Burrus, who died in March, A.D. 62. It was part of the duty of the Præfectus Prætorio to receive into his custody prisoners sent up to Rome from the provinces for trial.

16. ἐπετράπη, *permission was given.*

— στρατιώτῃ. This would be one of the Prætorian Guard, who would keep Paul in *custodia militaris.* See note on xxiv. 27.

17. πρώτους, *leading men,* in connexion perhaps with the Synagogues.

20. παρεκάλεσα, *I called you hither.*

— ἅλυσιν, *chain.* Observe the *singular,* and see xii. 6 ; xxi. 33.

22. ἀξιοῦμεν, *we think it right ;* as in xv. 38.

— ἃ φρονεῖς, *what opinions you hold.*

— αἱρέσεως, *sect.* See v. 17 ; xxiv. 14.

— ἀντιλέγεται, *it is spoken against.* See xiii. 45.

23. τὴν ξενίαν, *his lodging.*

— ἐξετίθετο, *gave an explanation ;* as in xi. 4.

23. διαμαρτυρόμενος, *solemnly testifying of*.

— πείθων, *teaching persuasively;* as in xix. 8.

25. ἀπελύοντο. Imperfect *middle, they dismissed themselves, they departed*.

25. Ἡσαΐου. Isaiah, the son of Amoz, prophesied in the reigns of Uzziah, Jotham, Ahaz, and Hezekiah, kings of Judah. He lived about 720 B.C. His name signifies *Salvation of Jehovah*. Of his life nothing is known. Tradition assigns to him martyrdom under Manasseh, king of Judah, by being sawn asunder.

27. ἐπαχύνθη, *waxed fat.* παχύνω means, *I make thick, I make fat,* and hence in the passive, *I grow fat.* Here it seems to be used for the heaviness and dulness accompanying excessive fatness.

— ἐκάμμυσαν, *they closed.* καμμύω is a poetic form of καταμύω, *to shut the eyes.* The simple μύω means *to close,* especially the eyes or the lips.

30. διετίαν, *a space of two years.* Probably from the spring of 61 A.D. to the spring of 63 A.D.

During the two years of St. Paul's imprisonment at Rome, it is considered certain that he wrote *four* Epistles; to the Philippians, the Ephesians, the Colossians, and Philemon.

According to the general opinion the Apostle was liberated from his imprisonment and left Rome, visited Greece, Asia Minor, and Spain, returned again to Rome, and was again imprisoned.

During this second imprisonment he wrote *three* Epistles ; two to Timothy, and the third to Titus.

A very ancient tradition, confirmed by the testimony of many ecclesiastical writers, relates that he was be-headed at Rome, about the same time that St. Peter was crucified there, in the reign of Nero, A.D. 68.—*Dict. of the Bible*, Art. PAUL.

www.ingramcontent.com/pod-product-compliance
Lightning Source LLC
Chambersburg PA
CBHW021108020726
47500CB00003B/656